ORPHAN PLANET

MADEEHAH REZA

LUNA NOVELLA #23

Luna Press PUBLISHING

For Ma, whose love for the moon and stars
is woven across these words.

Contents

Prologue

Her name is Elif, because she is the first of us to live on this world. You will do well to remind her of this name. Elif is just a baby, for now. She is a little pink thing that wriggles and squirms. Often she'll place her whole fist inside her mouth. It won't make sense, but you just need to keep her safe. There won't be any set instructions to stop her crying. You'll struggle at first, but I know you can figure it out because I'm going to help you do it. Babies can't be left alone. They'll roll and fall and drop and hurt themselves without realising and then start that racket all over again. There'll be a lot of this in the beginning. Trial and error, mostly error. Don't worry though, VAS-H. After a few years, Elif will become a girl.

Part One

Chapter One

— aged 12

Polaris did not contact Elif until her twelfth year of life. She sat cross-legged in her chair, skinny limbs covered in pyjamas too big for her. Dark, tangled hair fell across her round face. Elif's eyes widened when the woman's face filled the screen. She had seen humans before on films and shows, but they never looked directly at her. They were in their own worlds, not aware of the girl's existence. Now a whole human being had their attention solely on her. She shrunk in the chair as the Commander spoke to her.

"I am Commander Aremu of the Interplanetary Mission based on Polaris. I will be your contact with the Mission going forward."

Elif didn't know what any of that meant. Instead she focused on the Commander's smooth skin, which was as dark as the night sky. Her square jaw was all angles. Strands of the Commander's grey hair poked out from beneath a lopsided dark blue hat. Four gold stars twinkled from her right shoulder. Elif wanted to ask her what these meant, whether she could have a star too, but the words caught in her throat. The Commander did not explain why Polaris had not contacted her before this.

"Your first assignment, Warden, is to grow these plants and observe if they can grow on Maoira-I. Maoira-I is a planet of interest, and all planets of interest have a Warden like yourself."

VAS-H's mobile shell trundled towards the storage freezer behind Elif's chair, metal limbs squeaking as it retrieved several small packets, their outer coverings encrusted in ice. The girl took the packets absently, turning them over in her small hands. She had never seen these before. She wondered what else VAS-H knew that she didn't.

"And Warden," said the Commander. "You will always be addressed by senior members of the Mission. Should your appearance not be professional, they will not be happy."

"What does professional mean?" Elif also wanted to ask what 'warden' meant.

The Commander took a deep breath, the lines on her forehead tightening.

"Just make sure your hair is brushed, alright? Aremu signing out."

The screen went black. Elif saw the reflection of her hair in the shiny screen: thick and black and sticking out in several angles. Elif ran a hand through one side but several knots and tangles stopped her fingers. It hurt to keep going. Elif had never brushed her hair in her life.

"That was another person?"

"Correct," said VAS-H. "Commander Isobel Aremu. Leader of the Interplanetary Mission. The Mission seeks to find a new home for humanity."

Elif stared at the white packets in her hand for a while, trying to read the markings on them.

"What are these for?"

"As Warden of Maoira-I, you will have to perform various

assignments from the Mission. They will become longer and more difficult, but they always begin with growing plants."

"Why?"

"Because the planet needs to grow life. It will also test you to see if you are capable of such a commitment."

"What if I'm not?" Elif's voice grew quiet.

"You are," replied VAS-H. "You are already here, are you not?"

*

Elif sat in the recreation pod, watching a film. The pod was a round room with a long, circular sofa that went around the room's perimeter. Elif didn't like sitting on the sofa itself—it felt too big, too empty for her—so she took the square, grey seat cushions and placed a couple of them in a triangle with a blanket from her bunk thrown on top. She stared at the screen from her cushion tent, dark brown eyes dry from not blinking.

This film was about an underwater princess pursuing her dream of becoming a human with legs. There were several hundred shows to choose from on the Base's entertainment platform. Some of them were restricted from her, but she didn't care. She liked to rewatch the cartoons.

"Why is my name Elif?" she asked.

VAS-H activated its mobile shell, lights turning on in sequence. Sometimes VAS-H would stop working and Elif would have to work out how to bring the AI back to life. She figured that it needed an upgrade, but she didn't know how to go about this. She didn't know when Commander Aremu would contact her again for her to ask. *Next time*, she told herself, *I'll be braver.*

VAS-H's shell didn't have a face to be exact, but a jumble of repaired metal patches and cogs. In the centre, where the 'head' joined the central unit, was a silver voice box. VAS-H wheeled itself closer to Elif, who looked up when the AI's wheel got stuck to a piece of uneven flooring. She got up from her cushioned fortress and freed the wheel before fiddling with the floor until the offending piece broke off.

"This has always been your name," said VAS-H, its voice box glowing green. "A name is primarily needed for identification. Humans often have two: one is a given name and the other is a family name. This depends on the culture and traditions of the society that the human is from."

"What's a family?" asked Elif.

"A group of people related by a common ancestor."

She paused for a moment.

"Do I have a family?"

The question fed through VAS-H's pathways as it attempted to find the appropriate answer. Sometimes VAS-H would pause, take its time to answer the little Warden's questions. This annoyed Elif: why did VAS-H take so long? All it needed to do was reach into its database of knowledge and find the right answer.

"You have me," said VAS-H. "Because Polaris put both of us on this planet."

Elif thought about this, turning it over in her growing mind. "That means Polaris is our an… ancestor?"

VAS-H nodded and brought its rudimentary metal head down to look at the girl. Elif knew that the AI could still see the entire facility from its mobile shell; it didn't need to come closer to her to get a better look. But that wasn't why VAS-H brought its head down.

"Yes. We are family."

This seemed to satisfy the girl, so she slid back down to her cushions to watch the rest of the film.

MISSION LOG Maoira-I
MISSION 4B
Log: 01

Vash says that I have to document everything I do. I don't know what to write but Vash says I should do it so when I look back, I can see how far I've come.

We got a set of instructions from Commander Aremu, all the things she didn't have time to explain over the vidlink. It was a short list, like starting my lessons in Basic Physics, Plant Biology, Computer Coding, Self-First Aid. Aremu told me that I am the Warden of Maoira-I, so I had to look up what that meant:

n. warden [wawr-dn]
- someone who is in charge of or cares for or has custody over persons, animals or things; their keeper
- the highest executive officer in charge of a prison

That sounds like a lot of work. I've never looked after anything before. Vash looks after me, and sometimes I make sure Vash keeps working too.

Commander Aremu is the first human I've ever spoken to. She looks like an old lady, but I don't think I should tell her that. There are dark circles under her eyes that make her look very tired. What do others in Polaris look like? Is there anyone like me, or are they all old like Commander Aremu?

I didn't know we had a Garden in the Base. I thought it was just a storage room, around the corner from the infirmary. It's a square room and very white. There are four big lights in each corner but one of them is broken. I don't know how to fix it, but maybe Vash can show me. Vash teaches me everything.

Before dinner, we planted three different types of seeds and made a schedule for watering and feeding. I hope they grow quickly. I want to see what plants look like.

END OF LOG

Chapter Two

– aged 13

Elif climbed up a dirt hill and used a broken metal rod to hoist herself up the incline. In the late afternoon, the twin suns hid behind a swathe of dusty smog, their dim light washing across the land. It was warm yet the air felt thin, as if her lungs couldn't quite get enough into them. VAS-H told her to take a portable oxybox in case she needed it but Elif didn't listen. She regretted that now. She needed to preserve her energy to get back to the Base, so she had to stop at this hill. The readings from the control panel in the Base detected 19.8% oxygen in the atmosphere. It was safe enough to walk unaided without an oxybox or biosuit, but the control panel couldn't measure what it felt like walking for over an hour in a suboptimal atmosphere. That required human input, prior knowledge, a skilled interpretation of the data. Not for the first time since the Mission's contact was Elif swallowed by her vast inexperience. The Commander had assigned her the task of mapping out the immediate area surrounding the Base station, though she probably didn't realise how exhausting it was to travel across such a rocky land on foot. Had Aremu even stepped foot on a planet?

At the top of the hill, she stabbed a hole in the earth with the pole; a makeshift flagpole with a red cloth attached at the top. She needed a visual tool to keep track of how far she had gone because everywhere she looked was the same: dead trees, dead trees, dead trees. Hundreds of them, memories of a previous realm. Some had already fallen, half-buried into the ground, with no hint of green. Trees on Earth would grow moss on their bark even if they had no leaves, Elif had read. But the trees on Maoira-I were carcasses, devoid of life, beckoners of a frozen death.

This was the furthest Elif had walked from the Base in the past year and yet nothing in the landscape had changed. She threw her bag down and sat against a large, gnarled tree trunk atop the hill. It was a skeleton, like all the others, providing neither shade nor comfort. Inside the trunk was a hole, not carved by human hands, but forged from the insects of a bygone era. Elif poked her head inside to find it dry and placed herself comfortably inside. For a moment, she pictured herself as a woodland creature, like those in the cartoons she watched. She brought her tablet out from her satchel and made notes: the soil remained pale grey with sand-like texture and there was still that bitter taste in the air, as if she was breathing in metal. It was the first time she'd been out of the Base in fourteen days since Aremu's slew of new assignments, though it felt like more. Time seemed something she'd read about more than something that actually happened. The tree's roots were intertwined with the soil, spreading across the curvature of the hill. Roots as thick as her limbs, as gnarled as a witch's fingers. Elif brushed a hand across the root nearest to her, its rough surface scratching her skin. A loose piece of bark entwined with her fingers; she tugged gently, allowing it to come apart. The bark was thin, devoid of moisture, easy to snap. She placed it inside a sample container within her satchel before recording her findings. Elif drank from her canteen of water and surveyed the land around her.

This was the planet Maoira-I, and she was its keeper.

What a stupid name, she thought. The name meant nothing to her and she could find no reason for this particular choice in the Base's files. The planets in the primary star system— where humans had originated from—were given names based on mythology, of stories and legends from ancient history. She clicked the canteen closed and loosely swung its metal hook on her finger. What stories had taken place in this world? What legends could possibly have been told in a place so barren?

She pushed the thought from her mind and wondered if the repairs on VAS-H would take her all afternoon. Elif knew there would come a point when the updated protocols would outstrip the AI's pre-installed software. Then Elif would only have her own mind for company on a silent planet. Even the wind, when it did pick up, whistled quietly, barely a whisper in her ear.

The girl threw her canteen in her bag and dusted her hands off. She'd walk back to the Base for today before the evening fog settled in. Fog meant there was water somewhere on Maoira-I, but it was too high up to be useful.

Maybe fog water would help the plants grow, thought Elif as she swung the bag over her shoulder. More than a year had passed since Aremu's first assignment and not a single green stalk emerged from the soil. Without viable growth the planet would no longer be a candidate of Mission interest. Commander Aremu had rarely mentioned what would happen if that were the case; most of their conversations revolved around assignments and results. The bigger question of *what would happen if this planet was not habitable for human life*? hung in the ether between them. Would she be given a new planet to be a keeper over? What if she had to share her wardenship with another person? Elif paused on the latter thought as she skidded down the hill.

What a stupid idea.

*

"How was the scouting mission?" asked VAS-H. Elif stepped inside the outer airlock, a large empty room, larger than it needed to be for one person. She shrugged her bag off and placed its contents—her canteen and tablet and the sample containers—into a small receptacle that connected the outer and inner airlock. The bag she threw into a decontamination unit before stripping off her clothes and throwing them in the unit too. She raised her arms and closed her eyes as a fine mist sprayed across her entire body. Disinfectant. Once the process was complete, the edges around the large circular door lit up, now safe to open. Elif stepped inside the inner airlock and grabbed a fresh set of clothes from a nearby rack.

"Boring." Elif fished her canteen and tablet from the receptacle and switched the tablet on. "There's never anything out there."

The inner airlock doubled up as a workshop and had a large touchscreen which covered the northern wall while the opposite was decorated in dozens of drawers, containers and shelves. Inside these containers were things that might be needed to repair things around the Base, including VAS-H.

Elif connected the tablet to the large screen and flicked through the images she had taken. One was a timelapse video of the suns rising in a pale lavender sky. Elif squinted at the video, now larger, but still couldn't see any detail of interest.

"What am I even meant to be looking for?"

"You are not looking for anything. You are assigned to map the terrain." VAS-H's voice spread throughout the Base.

"I know that," she moaned. She stepped through the door from the workshop to the first hallway, bare feet slapping against the cold floor as she headed towards her dorm. "But why can't they just have a satellite do that? How far am I even meant to go?"

"A seven-mile radius in all directions, according to the report from Commander Aremu."

"Does she even know how long that takes to walk?" Elif stopped outside the door to the Garden. She stood on her tiptoes to look through the viewing port. It annoyed her that everything in the Base was designed for an adult, right down to the size of the doors. If they really wanted her to be the Warden, could they not have made it easier? The tips of her fingers turned white as she gripped the edge of the window and tilted her head to see as much as she could.

Three sunlamps flooded the Garden with sterile, white light. She still hadn't managed to fix the fourth lamp. The walls were covered in white tarp. At the centre were four rows, each with several mounds of fresh soil: the newest batch.

Elif peeked as much as she could before the arches of her feet ached.

"Still nothing," she whispered. "It's been two weeks."

"Patience, young Warden," came VAS-H's voice. "It takes a long time to grow."

Chapter Three

– aged 14

There was something buried deep in the soil, with only a metal edge sticking out. Elif was five miles out from the Base, oxybox in hand. The broken flagpole was her hiking stick as she climbed up a steep slope to the next landmark. Across the vast graveyard of twisted tree trunks sat the edge of a crater. There was no way to measure it, but she couldn't see the southern edge of the crater on the other side. The dark canyon stretched in front of her like a gaping, hungry mouth.

Elif wedged the pole where the soil was soft. The jagged edge hit something hard. Something that wasn't rock or stone or sand. She wiped the layer of dirt from the mysterious object to reveal a rectangular panel, like a window. What was a window doing in the ground? A thick layer of dried dirt covered it from the outside. There was still some water in her canteen, so she poured a little out and wiped the panel with her gloved hand. Elif pressed an eye to the glass but it was buried deep in the soil, too dark to see inside. She sat back and looked up at the overcast sky, now a muddy periwinkle. Windows didn't just appear from nowhere, they were created. They were manmade. Someone must have put this window here.

Her first instinct, as always, was to ask VAS-H, but of course the AI could not exist outside the Base. Even VAS-H's mobile shell was too fragile, too old to survive the safety of their home if it wasn't for Elif's repair jobs.

She had to figure out what this window was doing in the middle of the ground. Was it another Base, built into the side of a crater? Why had Aremu not mentioned this? Elif had nothing more than her tablet, canteen of water and a sachet of freeze-dried nuts and berries. And the broken flagpole, now tossed across the ground.

The flagpole. Elif grabbed it with both hands and steadied herself, wielding the pole like the shovel she used in the Garden.

She dug for a while. The suns were past their zenith, their circular outlines a faded glimmer behind the smog. Elif wiped the sweat off her brow and sat on the dusty ground. Even with all her might, she couldn't dig very far, but she'd scraped and uncovered enough for the window to evolve into the side panel of what seemed like a vehicle.

A vehicle. Something that could take her back to the Base and further afield for more exploration. How long had this been sitting here, covered in dirt? Perhaps it was defunct, perhaps an error or a mishap or an accident caused it to crash and become buried. But that meant someone else must have been here before Elif. Someone else must have been taking care of the planet.

*

Commander Aremu blinked on the screen. The dark patches under her eyes were ever-present, their colour deepening. Her face grew tighter with every vidlink meeting, jaw set and lips an unwavering line.

"I don't really understand what I'm supposed to be looking for," said Elif when asked about her scouting missions. "There's nothing out there except dead trees. And I can't walk that far; I get tired after about an hour."

The girl stared at her superior, watching as the lines in her face softened like melted clay. Suddenly she wanted to reach out into the screen and touch the Commander's face. She shook the thought away.

"That... that is understandable. But we are all counting on you, young Warden, to help us figure out if this is the planet for us to settle on. And if there are dead trees, that means they must have been alive at some point."

Elif tried to picture a life on the empty sands of this barren land, tried to see a home planted near the crater with small children playing. A sudden ache came over her, as if there was a great distance between her and that imaginary family.

"Are there other planets?" she asked. "Other choices?"

Aremu nodded. "But yours is the one we are most interested in. The climate conditions appear to be the most tolerable and sustainable for human life. Now, you wouldn't want to live on a frozen tundra, would you?"

Elif almost smiled as she pictured what such a planet would be like. To live like the arctic explorers of Old Earth—*that* would be an adventure. She shook her head.

"Very well. Please send a written report back to us via the portal with your results. I have some more assignments for you which you will find after this meeting. As always, you can find all the information you need with the VAS-H." Aremu paused for a moment, her mouth slightly open, as if hesitating on her next words.

"What was here before me?" She blurted out the words as soon as they had formed in her mind. "As in, were there other humans?"

Aremu blinked, this unwarranted question taking her by surprise. Her lips drew tight. "You are the Warden. You are the only human on Maoira-I."

"I know," said Elif, frustration bleeding into her voice. "But I didn't just come from nowhere. What about my parents?"

A pause came next before Aremu frowned. "Please keep the contents of these meetings strictly regarding your assignments."

Something snapped in Elif's chest, giving way to a molten hot fury. She wanted to shout at the older woman before she was interrupted.

"You know, I have a granddaughter about your age."

The girl sat up a little straighter, that red-hot thing in her chest melting away. "Really? What's her name?"

For a moment they stared at each other, held in a silence that was filled with something warm and easy; a world where there wasn't thousands of miles of empty space between two people. One where Elif might have been someone's granddaughter, with a name that sounded as sweet as honey on the tongue.

"Our meeting has concluded. This is Aremu signing out."

*

"VAS-H, remind me again what happened when you came here." Elif sat with her leg up on the seat, twirling her spoon in a bowl of grain porridge.

"Some years before you were assigned to me, I was installed to ensure all systems were up and running prior to a human Warden, to ensure safety checks were in place and to monitor any signs of atmospheric deterioration."

"And there was no one else here? No other humans have ever been on this planet?"

There was a pause. If VAS-H was human, Elif would think it was distracted.

"Before my installation, a crewed mission was sent from Polaris to Maoira-I to set up the Base over a few months. They would have been picked up by a return mission to Polaris once the Base was established."

So there were other humans, Elif thought, but they were long gone. That hollow ache from before grew, a weird feeling that made her feel unsteady from within. She knew she was physically fine, but it still hurt. A lot.

VAS-H continued without any prompt, "On other planets that are of interest to the Mission, my software would also have been installed. Our software would have been upgraded by the mission crew before they departed."

Elif looked up from her porridge. "What about me? I didn't come from the mission crew."

"No, you did not. I do not recall the reason for this, but it is certainly an anomaly to the protocol that was expected. It was a further ten years before I met you."

As she got ready for sleep, Elif wondered why she had been selected as the Warden. There wasn't anything remarkable about her that she was aware of, but then again she was the only other person she'd ever known. Did the other Wardens think the same thing, marooned on their planets?

Her mind was tired and fuzzy and full of thoughts that would never be answered. It was a heavy thing to go to bed with, every night.

MISSION LOG Maoira-I
MISSION 4B
Log: 187

I've dug out the vehicle completely. It took me about a month. I wonder how long it's been buried under the soil for, and how it got there? Did it just stop working, or was it forgotten about? I've never driven a vehicle before. There's never been a reason for me to go so far out from the Base.

I'm going off-assignment here. Aremu doesn't know about this and I don't want to tell her. I don't think she'd approve. But it's... nice. It's nice having something that's all my own. Something that isn't protocol or authorised. This is my unauthorised experiment. And tomorrow, I'm going to try and drive the vehicle back to Base.

Assignments from Commander Aremu:
- Commence blood deposits in infirmary (weekly finger-prick blood tests)
- Commence monthly urine and stool sample deposits in infirmary
- Continue scouting missions within 10-mile radius of Base; make note of important landmarks, possible/past sources of water, take soil samples where possible
- Examine new soil samples in Laboratory for any signs of bacterial life form
- Continue lessons in Level 2 Botany incl. Basics in Botanical Chemistry, Fundamental Meteorology, Advanced Mathematics, Basics of Energy & Entropy, Advanced Laboratory Techniques

- Monitor plant growth in Garden & use available soil collections in the depository
- Try not to interrupt Mission officials when they speak

END OF LOG

Polaris

—Jaflong District, Aremu compound

Isobel Aremu sat in her garden, a glass of cool lemonade on the deck table next to her, with a book in hand. An artefact from a bygone era, it was a family heirloom, a relic from Old Earth. Her fingers caressed the book's spine but her eyes merely glazed over the pages. The black lines of text were incomprehensible; the pages had faded terribly. If she'd handed this over to the archivists, they may have restored it to some fraction of its former glory. But Isobel was not particularly concerned with what the text might have said. She did not care whether it was fact or fiction or something in between. What mattered was that it came from Earth. She needed that reminder.

"Hey Grams." Esther swung around her grandmother's chair and planted a kiss on her forehead. "What you reading?"

"Nothing," said Isobel, placing the book aside. "How was school?"

Esther pulled her face into a frown and held it until her grandmother laughed.

"Come on, let's get dinner ready."

As Esther regaled her with tales of the latest trends at school, Isobel caught her finger on the hot stove. She ran it under cold water absently, Esther's words floating in and out of her ears, her mind fluttering back to the book still on the garden table. She wondered if another planet in this vast universe would be enough for humans, enough for their needs and desires and vices, enough to create a book with pages thin enough to give stinging papercuts.

A bell rang throughout the house. Esther rushed to the front door where muffled noises could be heard. Isobel dried her hands off and went to inspect the hushed commotion. The office knew better than to disturb her at home.

"Who is it Esther?"

Her granddaughter stepped away. A man stood at the front door, thin and wiry with skin like the sheets of paper in her book. Behind him was a woman with dark glasses and a broadcasting camera hung over her shoulder.

Isobel straightened up immediately, gently pushing Esther away from the door. "If this about the Return To Earth protests, all media enquiries will need to go through the Mission's press office."

"Mrs Aremu—" *began the man.*

"Commander *Aremu.*"

He paused before nodding. A small microphone was clipped below the collar of his shirt. "Commander Aremu, there are a number of protests regarding the ethics of the Mission—"

"Young man, as I said, all enquiries must be directed to—"

"We have evidence to suggest that the Mission, under your direction and command, has approved of keeping an unaccompanied minor on a deserted planet that is no longer of interest to the Mission. Can we confirm if this is true?"

Isobel shut the door. Esther asked her what was wrong. Isobel shouted back, telling her granddaughter to go to her room.

Chapter Four

"There is an incoming message. Your next Assignment Day will be in twenty-four hours. You are expected to compile a brief report of—"

"Of my findings and observations, *I know*."

The only surprising thing about Assignment Day was the timing. It wasn't that she had other pressing matters to attend to, but Elif wished there was some method to the Mission's contact. Some part of her wished they contacted her more often.

"I've got a surprise for you." Elif called out to the AI from where she perched on the workshop bench, flicking through images on her tablet. VAS-H did not have access to the contents of the tablet. The tablet was a portable way to access the Base's files, so there was never a reason for giving the AI access to it. But this also meant VAS-H could not read the additional files of Elif's logs.

"A surprise?" said VAS-H's disembodied voice. "Define, 'surprise'."

Elif sighed. "Never mind. I'm going for another walk; I'll be back later."

"Young Elif," started the AI. "You need to begin your feedback report. It usually takes you on average two hours and forty-six minutes to complete it."

Elif waved her hand in the air, eyes fixated on the images of the vehicle. A dirt-ridden and damaged enigma, but she was so close to uncovering it completely.

"I'll do it later," she muttered.

"Your recent explorations outside the Base have taken you an average of six hours and twelve minutes. If it takes this long today, you likely won't be back with enough time and energy to complete your report."

She switched her tablet off and stuffed it into her bag. "I don't need you to tell me what to do. *I'm* the Warden, not you."

The AI stayed quiet. Elif swung her bag around her shoulder and made for the inner airlock door before its frame, normally illuminated with a soft white, turned dark.

"VAS-H, open the door, now. You know you can't do these things without my permission."

"I did not lock the door," said the AI. "It is an automatic override that takes place when a significant atmospheric change is detected."

Barely a second after VAS-H spoke, the Base filled with a high-pitched beep. Elif wasted no time in explanations; the protocol was drilled into her muscles. She ran from the workshop back to the control room off the first hallway. Her heart thudded louder but not faster. She knew what to do.

A large computer with four screens and keyboards sat inside the control room, all monitoring the Base and its surroundings. It was also the room where she spoke to Aremu on Assignment Day.

"I don't understand," muttered Elif, reading the meteorological data that flashed on the screen. "There's been a drop in atmospheric pressure. The temperature's lowered too.

This is... this has been consistent for years. How did I miss this?"

"It may be unwise to continue your exploration trip," said the AI.

Elif shook her head.

"No, oxygen and CO2 are still acceptable." The weather was changing without a clear reason, and Elif knew she wasn't going to find the reason sitting in the Base and writing a report. She spent another few minutes at the keyboard, fiddling with the interior commands of the Base's security files. "I've disabled the automatic override for now. I'll be back soon."

*

Elif had spent the last hour attempting to pry open the door to the vehicle, but it would not budge. She could find no instructions on her tablet either; there was no folder called 'mysterious vehicle'. One continuous window ran along the front and sides; she could break it but any damage would probably work against her in the long run. It had large rubber wheels, almost the same height as Elif, which she leant against as she carried all her tension in her fists. Elif took a deep breath and then out, uncurling her hands in time. She tried not to cry. That never solved anything. She had been told as much by Commander Aremu some months ago, before she'd turned fourteen.

The sky remained a blanket of smog. Grey skies were more common now, their dullness depressing into her bones. Elif missed the violet sky, but she refused to cry over that either. A chill breeze scratched against her arms and she suddenly wished she had brought a jacket. Everything felt wrong, everything was going wrong. The girl pressed her thumb and forefinger against her eyelids, as if she could push the tears back into their ducts.

"Why won't you open?" She spun around and kicked the edge of the large tyres before placing her palms on the dirty metal body. "And where did you come from?"

A faded smudge appeared beneath her gloved hand. She wiped the surface several more times to uncover bold, black words: *Transporter Z-42*. And just beneath the words was an image: two circles looping over each other, housing a seven-pointed star inside them. The logo of the Interplanetary Mission. Elif took a step back, her heart *thud-thud-thudding*, before wiping more of the dirt off with her hands. There were no other words, no other signs.

The Mission must have made this for the set-up crew. Maybe it detected the atmosphere's change too… maybe it has an automatic lock system. It would need to keep the operator of the vehicle safe, like the Base had done for her. *But there has to be some kind of safety mechanism… it's stupid to be trapped inside a locked vehicle.*

She walked around the perimeter and surveyed the vehicle from all sides before clambering onto its hull. Once she reached the top panel, the first one she'd uncovered, she traced the edges for any groove or lock that she could break open. And, at last, there it was. A small opening, large enough for three adult fingers to pull the discreet lever. Elif used her whole hand to yank the lever open. The panel opened out and left an entrance wide enough for her to drop into. Once she fell on the seat inside, a plume of dust rose upwards.

Several buttons were at her command, displayed in front of her like another control panel. The panels were split in half by a steering wheel, its rim too thick for Elif to grasp comfortably. A single pedal sat a few inches from her feet, and she knew from her movies that pedals made cars go faster. Elif tried to press it but it was too far away; she slipped down the seat and pushed it with her foot, but nothing happened. A slim lever with a dark blue ball stuck out on her left-hand side. Next to it, a black screen was embedded into the control panel. Where did she even begin?

The sky darkened overhead as the thick evening fog rolled on the ground, thicker than she'd seen before. Was this part of the weather changing? She'd never make it back safely on foot, not now she could barely see a few feet in front of her. Elif ran her hands over the buttons, listening to the soft clatter beneath her fingers, and placed both hands on the steering wheel. If the pedal couldn't kick the vehicle into motion, what else would there be? Some kind of ignition key? She placed a hand on the shift lever and pulled it backwards. Nothing happened.

"Come on, this is like any other problem." She squeezed her eyes shut, absently pushing the lever forwards. The vehicle lurched. Elif snapped back up and stared at the lever. It would not go any further forward in its groove. She placed it back in the neutral position before pushing it forward again. Once again, the Transporter lurched, as if it wanted to move but was missing a key ingredient.

"So this must make you go forward once the vehicle switches on," she muttered to herself. "But where is the 'on' button..."

A green warning fluttered on the black screen to her right.
          IGNITION REQUIRED — YES / NO
The girl stared at the screen for a second before tapping 'Yes'.

The engine roared behind her, a thunderstorm inside a metal cage. She clutched her ears tightly before relaxing her shoulders as the engine came to a steady hum. Elif placed a wary hand on the lever and gently pushed forwards.

The Transporter rolled ahead.

*

The Transporter moved smoothly across the uneven terrain of the valley. Its large wheels absorbed the shocks and bumps that made walking tiring. But it was noisy, and that annoyed Elif. The engine would not stop grating behind her, and with the sound came vibrations that shook her in the driver's seat.

Travelling across the fog didn't need *her* eyes; the screen was also a navigator, its dark background filled with constellations that spread themselves across Maoira-I's sky like spilled sugar. Elif had never seen the skies without their grey shroud of clouds. The fog ahead of her was illuminated by several circular headlights, but Elif leaned forwards to look at the sky. She tried to picture the stars above her. What other planets would be across the way? Was this where the fleet of ships were anchored in zero-gravity, just beyond the veil of clouds—

The Transporter jolted, throwing Elif forwards, her abdomen crushing into the steering wheel. She gripped the rim of the wheel and pushed herself back into the seat, gasping for air. The Transporter was still moving, but moving far too fast. She reached out for the lever and pulled it back to its central position, but the vehicle kept rolling through the fog.

She was on the slope towards the Base and heading down fast.

Nothing happened when she pulled the lever backwards.

The end of the slope was approaching. Several dead tree trunks lined the terrain ahead; she would crash into one of them and flip over. She clutched the steering wheel and leant forwards, squeezing her eyes shut as the adrenaline pounded against her skull. She didn't want to see it when it happened. She tried to picture the Base, safe and warm, but only Commander Aremu's face came to mind, Aremu's dark eyes and tight-lipped mouth and how she was the only human that Elif had ever known and how pathetic and sad that was—

Her foot brushed against the single pedal. Elif shot up and looked straight ahead. She slipped down the seat, stretching a leg to push the pedal down, just a little closer...

The Transporter jerked to a stop and threw her into the windshield like a ragdoll. Elif hit the glass and rolled into the gap between the windshield and control panel. For the briefest of moments, Elif imagined Aremu's disappointment before falling into a deep and silent blackness.

Chapter Five

The ringing came first. A constant chaos in her ears that became louder as her eyes fluttered open. The early morning sky was fractured by dark lines, a clear pool of pale lavender splintered into jagged pieces.

Elif raised a hand to the sky to feel its fragments. Her fingertips brushed against cold glass. The windshield was broken. The Transporter was blaring an alarm into her ears. Her ribs burned and back ached and shoulder was bruised and she didn't know where she was or what time it was or why the sky was so bright—

"Assignment Day," she whispered. Elif hauled herself back up, wincing at the cacophony of muscles crying out in pain. The Transporter had, somehow, landed right-side up. She shuffled off the control panel and stared at its buttons, trying to make sense of the alarm and how to switch it off. A warning flashed on the black screen.

BATTERY LOW
BATTERY SAVING MODE REQUIRED — YES/NO

She tapped 'No' hazily, still in a daze. The screen turned black once more and finally, there was silence. Elif nudged the door open with her good shoulder and jumped off the

Transporter. The cold morning air greeted her with prickles across her skin. The aches across her body felt worse as she walked, but she knew she was running late. Elif broke into a sprint.

*

The decontamination process in the outer airlock was taking a lifetime. Elif's heart hammered against her bruised ribs. She stood with restless limbs and closed her eyes against the spraying.

"Young Warden, you are late," came VAS-H's voice from overhead.

"I know," she said through gritted teeth. The bitterness of the disinfectant bled into her mouth.

"The vidlink has already started."

The edges around the airlock door lit up. The girl ran through, getting dressed quickly, nearly tripping over her own feet as she stumbled through to the control room.

A pale face filled the screen. A man sat back on a black couch, its soft material shining in the light of his room. He wore the same uniform as Commander Aremu but with three gold stars on his shoulder instead of four. He had no beret, nothing on his head to hide his cropped blond hair. His pale skin was unblemished by anything except a patch of fuzzy hair brushed between his nose and mouth. Elif froze as she stared back at him. Her hand gripped the back of the chair.

"Who are you?" Elif didn't wait for an introduction. "Where's Commander Aremu?"

"Warden, you are very late. And why do you seem like you've run through a battleground?"

Elif found herself looking away from the man; his eyes were too light, too bleached, too open. She could see the blacks of their pupils. His voice was deeper than Aremu's but smoother, the edges of his words sharp like cut glass. Elif didn't know what he meant. She squeezed the chair tighter, her jaw set.

"Who are you?"

The man sighed in disappointment.

"I am Lieutenant Bishop. I'll be your contact with the Mission going forwards. Commander Aremu is... well, no longer Commander. But that's not your concern, is it Warden?"

Elif was ready to run. Why did she feel so unsettled? There was nothing this man could do to her. He was millions of miles away, wherever the fleet of ships were. But she didn't like the way his eyes widened, or the way his thin lips curled at the edges. She didn't like his excuse of a moustache either.

She said nothing. Lieutenant Bishop coughed and raised a hand in front of the camera, gesturing at the chair. "Why don't you sit down, Warden? Then we can have a proper chat."

It wasn't a question, so the girl did as she was told.

When the silence lingered between them, Bishop continued to speak. "Well, you might want to start by explaining why you are–" he checked a silver band tied to his wrist, "–eighteen and a half minutes late?"

"I was distracted by my assignments," she blurted out, having had the excuse ready for Aremu. "The plants in the Garden aren't growing. I've tried several soil compositions, different watering and light regimens–"

"I was under the impression that the Base's AI would remind you about Assignment Day." Bishop had no qualms talking over Elif. She stared at him, this time directly at his strangely light-coloured eyes, and frowned.

"Yes. The AI did tell me. I chose to ignore it."

"Well, that's not good, is it?" She wasn't sure if she should respond. Bishop scratched his bare chin. "We may need to look into your AI and see if it needs fixing."

"I do fix it," she said, again too quickly. "I make sure it keeps going, even though the software is seriously outdated." It was meant as a dig at the Mission: *hey, look at me, keeping this place running by myself.*

Bishop's eyes widened imperceptibly. Elif shifted in her seat.

"Impressive, Warden, but that seems unnecessary. I think we should just scrap the whole AI altogether. Give you something a little more upgraded, eh? You wouldn't even need to do your assignments. The AI would do most of the work."

Elif shook her head before she realised she was doing it.

Bishop smirked. "That's always the case. People get too attached to their AIs." He took a deep breath and closed his eyes for a few moments too long. Elif wondered if he was going to sleep on the screen. Then he opened them again and held his fingers in a loose triangle shape. "Go on then. Tell me about your little garden."

Elif steeled herself. She hadn't finished compiling her report, but she knew her assignments like the back of her hand.

"Like I said, nothing grows. The Base's supply of stored soil was low, so I gathered some more from the surrounding areas. The ground around the Base is desiccated and too dry for any nutrients, but the soil from further away seems soft to touch. I planted the last set of seeds a week ago with this." Bishop nodded, and she felt a flip inside her chest, as if his approval meant something to her, like Aremu's did. She shivered the feeling away. "So I guess we'll see in a few days if this batch grows or not."

She kept quiet, looking away from Bishop.

"This is the important one then, isn't it?" he said finally. "Because if this batch doesn't grow, then what *are* we going to do with you?"

Her throat grew dry. She didn't like the way Bishop spoke, as if she was a piece in a puzzle to be moved around. Like the environmental factors in the Garden that could be tweaked and adjusted to fit the experiment's outcome. She moved the conversation forwards, ignoring the gnawing sensation at the pit of her stomach.

"I've scouted around the Base for a nine-mile radius. There's nothing out there, just dead trees and dead land."

Bishop nodded. "It seems that there is death everywhere for you."

Elif's throat went dry, unsure how to respond to this. "There's nothing growing now, but there is obvious evidence there used to be life. It's hard to tell if this will come back, and it's possible the planet goes through long seasons, much longer than what Earth had. As there are two suns and with the axial tilt—"

"We are aware of these planetary parameters," said Bishop sharply. "And the atmosphere?"

"Still breathable. The composition is similar to Earth's, though there was a significant reduction in pressure yesterday. There's been a downward trend for some years. It might be the start of seasonal variation."

Bishop considered this. "Tell me more about the seasons."

"I think—I mean, I predict," said Elif, using the words Aremu had taught her when presenting a report, "the seasons will shift in the next couple of years. From there we can see if anything grows. The terrain itself is rocky, difficult to walk across." She paused for a moment, slowly meeting Bishop's gaze again. His had not wavered. "If only there was some way to transport myself across the land."

The Lieutenant was unfazed. "This is good work, Warden. I can see why Aremu was so invested in this planet, and in you."

Elif paused. Her heart expanded, filling itself with warmth from somewhere.

"The Commander was invested in me?"

Bishop nodded casually, his focus on something behind the camera. He seemed bored of their conversation. "Yes, she was."

If she didn't ask now, she'd never find out. "What... what happened to her?"

Bishop straightened up on the couch and fiddled with the buttons on his uniform. "She retired. Wanted to spend more time with her family. A shame, isn't it? She was a fine Commander. For the most part. I have some news, Warden. We want to add to your research team —" Elif nearly scoffed, her research team was just her, "—so we're sending you some assistance."

"Another AI?"

"No, another person. A companion of sorts."

Elif sat back in her chair. It would mean rationing the food, sectioning off the dormitories for them. Sharing her space. A whole other human being living with her, breathing the same air. She imagined someone like Bishop walking about the Base, poking into her experiments and assignments. Leaving footprints in the Garden. Her insides tightened at the thought.

"I can manage all my assignments myself, haven't I shown that?"

"It's not that, Warden. We are very interested in Maoira-I, so we're sending you a skilled engineer to help you with your assignments and, hopefully, speed up the process of finding a new planet."

"You can't speed up observations. They take time."

Bishop ignored her. "You can expect your helper to arrive in the next few years. We will have more accurate details ready nearer the time. Bishop signing—"

"What's their name?"

Bishop blinked at her.

"I don't know. We haven't selected them yet." He lazily waved a hand at someone behind the camera. "We've routed another resource package that should arrive planetside, some kilometres away from the Base, within a few weeks. We'll send coordinates of its landing location in due course. Bishop, signing out."

Chapter Six

Elif stayed in the control room after Bishop signed off. She pulled up a climate report and scanned the figures of atmospheric pressure, mean temperature during the day and night, the wind direction and speed.

Probably only a couple of weeks before I have to stay inside… for how long? There was the exo-suit, but she was still too short to fit into it. That was a Mission oversight that always bothered her—what was the point of making her the Warden without anything being her size? She had a few more days to get the Transporter back to Base before she was potentially in lockdown.

Her stomach grumbled. She hadn't eaten since the day before. A layer of dirt, sweat and blood coated her skin. Normally she'd be itching for a shower but now she just wanted to get back to the Transporter. Elif silently cursed herself for being a human with ridiculously mundane needs.

"Elif," began VAS-H from overhead. "Yesterday you set the manual override to continue scouting outside. Then you were very late to your assignment briefing today. You also appear to be injured. Can you provide an explanation for this?" There was nothing accusatory in its tone, no hint of malice. It was a simple question that required a simple answer to ensure the safety of the Warden. Elif walked through the Base's lit hallways, trying not to wince as the pain below her ribs grew louder with every breath. She bit the inside of her cheek.

"I wish I could show you."

"I do not understand your response."

The kitchen was a square room lined with light grey cupboards, a motion-activated sink, a stovetop and an automatic washing unit. In the centre was a circular grey table with five cushioned chairs. It always felt like a room that was too big for its occupant.

Elif raised her voice. "I made a discovery, Vash. I found a vehicle out near the crater. I even had to dig it out. But I drove it all the way back here—well, nearly, I sort of crashed it—but I'm figuring out how to use it! It's so close to the Base now, probably a kilometre or so away. I'm going to go back out to get it just as soon as I've eaten."

They're all nearly empty, thought Elif as she opened each cupboard, searching for a breakfast pack. The Mission's resource package was on its way so she could finally restock her supplies. They sent the packages twelve times in a year. For a brief moment, Elif wondered what would happen if they ceased to send them to her. How would she get food? She shook the thought away, instead wondering if the new 'helper' would know more. She didn't like that thought either.

"A vehicle?" VAS-H asked.

Elif poured a pack of instant porridge into a bowl and stirred in hot water. "Yeah, it's called the Transporter."

There was another pause before VAS-H finally said, "I do not have any records of an actively working Transporter."

"What do you mean?"

"The last functional Transporter lost connection with the Base thirteen years and four months ago."

The porridge was flavourless—she'd already eaten all the tasty ones—but Elif couldn't do much until the next batch arrived. She chewed the hot gruel before reluctantly swallowing.

"That was when the set-up crew was here, right? I wonder why they abandoned it instead of bringing it back to Base."

"I do not know. This information should be stored in our databases, but I cannot find anything."

VAS-H's words floated around her. She paid them no attention as her thoughts focused on the Transporter, and how to charge its battery. She'd have a search of the vehicle's files in the database first, to ascertain what happened nearly fourteen years ago, and then look up its user manual, find the *proper* controls on how to navigate it, find out what all the buttons on its control panel meant, find—

"Elif, it is time for you to check on the Garden. Remember, this assignment is of the highest priority."

The girl placed her used bowl into the washing unit drawer. "Later, Vash."

"Young Warden, I cannot stress how much importance the Mission has placed—"

"I said *later*. The Mission isn't here, is it? It's just you and me. So let's do what *we* want to do for a change."

*

There were two spare batteries stored in the workshop. They were inside an unlabelled container on a back shelf, each battery as long as Elif's arm. On pressing the 'CHARGE

SUPPLY' button on both, a small green light appeared. They were fully charged.

Elif found the Transporter's manual in the vast array of documents in her tablet, easier to find now she knew its name. She sat down inside the vehicle, her short legs dangling out the door, and flicked through the manual to find out how to drive it properly, the second task after she had learned how to replace the battery. The Transporter was well insulated if she kept the door shut, but it shouldn't have been this cold in the first place. The change in weather was an anomaly that didn't seem to stop; no longer a deviation, but a pattern. She should have seen it coming, though, if she'd paid attention to the weather data. But she wasn't a meteorologist. She wasn't a mechanic or a botanist or a medic or a comms specialist—

"Stop it," she snapped at herself. "I can be anything I want to be." She rubbed the tears away from her eyes and focused on the words in front of her.

It seems the Transporter was not only used for transport, but for the assignments and experiments themselves. There were tubes that could collect samples from the soil, a pop-up camera on the upper hull that could take a panoramic shot of the landscape and even an autopilot function to drive from point A to B. Mini solar panels covered the back of the hull, which would have been useful if the sky wasn't now perpetually covered in clouds. And solar power from two suns? She could have covered greater distances, perhaps even made discoveries that were far more interesting than an empty Garden where no plants grew. *Somewhere out there, there are trees that are alive.*

It did not take long to drive the Transporter back to Base once she knew how to navigate herself properly (and had brought a couple of cushions to prop herself forward against the seat to comfortably reach the brake pedal). A diagram in the manual's appendix showed how the Transporter was meant to be parked safely inside the outer airlock and set to charge its battery.

The airlock's door had always been wide. It opened by sliding upwards into the outer wall. Elif had never questioned just how wide the airlock was; ever since finding out about the set-up crew, she just assumed it was to fit more than one person inside the decontamination unit. Now she could see, as she slowly eased the Transporter inside the airlock, that it fit the vehicle's height perfectly. She braked gently and set the vehicle into neutral before switching it off and sliding off into the room. A wave of discomfort washed through her, as if she was an outsider in someone else's home. It made no sense— this was her home. But why was she discovering new things about it now?

"Hello Elif. I see you have brought the Transporter back to us," came VAS-H's voice.

"I have. Is there a way you can run diagnostics on it?"

"There should be an extendable cable just above the rear wheel. You can plug that into the vehicle outlet on the right hand side of the airlock."

Once she had done as much, and cycled herself through the decontamination process, Elif looked upon the large screen inside the workshop. An array of numbers and sequences sped down the black screen, too fast for her to read or interpret.

"The diagnostic report will be ready in an hour," said VAS-H.

Elif nodded and turned to leave before VAS-H spoke overhead once more. "There is something blocking the circuits in the dashboard. The report cannot continue until this is dealt with."

"But I didn't even touch it... I just followed instructions on how to drive." Elif raced back to the vehicle, knowing she'd have to go through the hassle of decontaminating again. She pulled herself up using the handrails and climbed inside the Transporter.

"It is a missing connection. I cannot continue unless this is fixed."

Elif felt around the surface of the dashboard, but there was nothing untoward. She fell on her back and slid across the floor beneath the dashboard panel, trying to look for an obstruction in the dim light.

"There it is," she said, "it's an extra wire that's not been connected. One sec." Once the problem was solved, she slid back out before something hard and sharp pinched her back. She scrambled up, thinking she'd broken another piece of equipment, before she saw a small but thick silver ring. Where had it come from?

"Is everything alright, Elif?"

"All good," she said as she slid out of the vehicle. In the light of the airlock, she held the ring out. The silver was dull, probably from age, but the thing that glistened was the large, orange gem in its middle. She turned it over in her palm. On one side was a hard substance, dark red and tarry. It flaked off as she picked at it. A red stain spread across her fingernail.

"Oh, ew! It's blood!"

"What is blood?" asked VAS-H.

"It was stuck to the floor with blood! That's... that's weird. And gross."

"Are you sure it is blood?"

Elif nodded. "I've fallen over and cut myself enough times to know what it is."

"One hundred and forty-two times, to be exact."

Elif glared at the ceiling.

"But you are right. That is an anomaly," said the AI before it encouraged the young girl to get some rest.

MISSION LOG Maoira-I
MISSION 4B
Log: 289

Amber is a precious gem. It's made from the resin that comes from trees. Resin is a substance produced by tree cells when the plant gets injured. It hardens when exposed to the air, to the outside environment. It hardens over the injury, creating a bandage of sorts, protecting the tree from further harm. Like its own little infirmary.

Either the gem on this ring is fake or it's come a long way to be made from trees. And who does it even belong to? VAS-H doesn't know. And why's there blood all over it? I wish I could analyse the blood, like on those crime shows I'm too young to watch. Yeah, I managed to break the age restriction on the media files. It really wasn't difficult.

Also, here's a thing I found interesting while studying:

The Three Decade Restoration Directive is an artificial intelligence protocol within all fleet ships (Polaris, Vesteris, Mathilas... etc.) to ensure up-to-date software and removal of any corruptions from a closed system. After thirty years of use, an AI will permanently and irreversibly shut down. There is no override for this function. Any persons attempting to override the Restoration Directive will a) find their attempts futile and b) pay a fine to the Ministry of Legislation.

Conclusion: I've found a new challenge.

END OF LOG

Chapter Seven

– aged 15

They really don't know good music. Elif perused the data files that were sent with the latest resource package. She thought about who picked the media files to send to her—the music, films, documentaries and books—and wondered if any of them were fifteen years old. Most likely not.

"Vash, there's something here for you," she called out as she scanned another document. "Seems like they've accepted my request for a stabilisation patch. They've sent it in the upgraded code."

"And this will help you with your assignments?"

Elif stretched her arms above her head, yawning as she spoke. "Of course. I can send you out in the field now, especially when the weather finally caves us in."

It had been one year since she first noticed the change in atmospheric readings. Elif checked the oxygen and carbon dioxide levels every day, almost obsessively, but the readings remained stable. There was no dip, no significant change. But she knew it couldn't stay like this for long. Twelve years ago, and then again eight years ago, there was a similar pattern—a sharp drop, followed by a period of stabilisation. It would only take another sharp drop for the planet's atmosphere to become unlivable for a human, and then Elif would be isolated inside the walls of the Base. But that didn't mean she couldn't still venture outside even if *she* had to stay inside.

She tapped a key on the keyboard and played a new song from the media file folder. A strong bass filled the air, followed by a guitar riff.

"Now *this* is much better," she said, spinning her chair around. "Hey Vash, do you like music?"

"I have neither a like nor a dislike for musical entertainment. It is the same with films," came the voice overhead. Elif nodded as she bobbed her head in time to the beat, though a part of her grew smaller. It was hard to explain, hard to even write in her logs, that every time VAS-H made it clear that it was an AI and not like a human in the slightest, Elif felt the disconnect between them grow larger. She wondered if there was even a connection in the first place, or had she just imagined it?

"So you don't like any kind of entertainment then?"

A pause, probably a skitter of code in the Base's central processor as VAS-H searched for the most accurate answer.

"Define 'entertainment'."

Elif sighed and swivelled back to the keyboard, looking up the word in her digital dictionary.

"'*Entertainment. A noun. Providing or being provided with amusement or enjoyment.*'" She braced herself against the question of defining 'amusement' or 'enjoyment'.

There was another pause. "I enjoy talking to you, Elif."

The girl sat up straight, frowning. "But that's not entertainment! I'm not like a book you can read."

"You provide me with enjoyment."

The AI's answer made no sense, but Elif could not dwell on it. It was the start of another Assignment Day, and this time she had her report ready. Bishop wasn't going to catch her out on any mistakes this time, not since he had done four months ago when he discovered she had been working on the Transporter. Secretly she was amused by the way his moustache had bristled as he listened to how she dug out the vehicle and brought it back to life. She switched on the vidlink and waited for the connection, quickly checking her hair was brushed in the black waiting screen. Then Bishop's face filled the screen.

"Hello, Commander Bishop." Elif hated how her voice wobbled. She was also not used to calling him by his new title and ignored the familiar ache that settled in the pit of her stomach, hollow yet painful. She missed Commander Aremu.

Bishop stepped back from the camera and sat down. There were several other people sitting around a table, some men and women.

Elif froze. She wanted to switch the camera off. There were too many people, completely new humans whom she had no introduction to, no idea what they were like. The contents of her stomach roiled and threatened to burn up to her throat. Her chest heaved.

"Warden," came Bishop's voice from the far end of the table. "This is the board committee. We thought it would be a good time to introduce you to others in the Mission staff." He spoke some more, the words washing over her ears. Elif could barely bring her eyes to meet his, let alone the people that sat around him. They all wore the same uniform, but their faces were featureless. "Seeing as you have proven yourself to be *quite* capable, we are interested in moving forward to investigate Maoira-I. Now, the weather reports..."

Elif shook her head and stared below the screen. She breathed in short, sharp bursts.

"Can you hear me?" came Bishop's voice from far, far away. "Jimoh, check the connection." A silence came over the meeting as someone left the table and shuffled behind the camera. There was some muttering before Bishop resumed talking.

"There's too many people," she blurted out. "Too many people. I can't do this." She switched off the vidlink.

Her head swam underwater, heavy and muted. Her face felt hot. She wanted to lie down. She wanted to cry. Instead she blasted *The Corrosive Brothers'* song, placing her head on the desk and tried to shut everything out, tapping her feet in time to the music.

*

Elif did not want to talk about what had happened in the meeting. The oblivious AI asked anyway as she knelt in the Garden, digging pits into the ground for the fourth time that week. She had collected soil samples in a fifteen-mile radius around the Base at half-a-mile increments. This was her fourth batch from that group of samples: twenty rows of planted seeds, each with a place card to identify their name and species. The previous batch, another twenty rows, lay as dormant piles of soil on the right side of the Garden.

"You left the meeting early. Was there a problem? Commander Bishop has requested your presence at a rescheduled meeting later this week."

"I don't want to talk about it," she said quietly. And she didn't want to see Bishop's face again.

"It will be a one-to-one meeting, as Commander Bishop had noted your apprehension—"

"I *said*, I don't want to talk about it."

"Is there something the matter, young Warden?" VAS-H was now in its metal shell. It held a bucket of gardening tools in its metal grip: a shovel, trowel and a small watering can. Earth tools.

Elif twisted a cream-coloured place card into the soil. *Oryza sativa, Poaceae family*. Rice.

"Why won't he call me by my name?" she asked quietly. "Aremu never did that either. Is 'Elif' actually my name?"

VAS-H did not reply. Another pile of soil, another seed buried deep. Another place card. *Solanum tuberosum, Solanaceae family*. Potatoes.

"Everyone has a name," Elif said softly. "Even you do, Vash."

"My name is an abbreviation of my function. *Vital*—"

"I know, I know." She took the watering can from VAS-H's hand. "*Vital Auxiliary Support: H-unit*. But at least you're called by your name." She sprinkled water across the newly planted mounds.

"Is it important to call you 'Elif', young Warden?"

She looked up at the AI's shell, staring at the place where there should have been eyes. Instead there was a blank strip of metal. She wanted VAS-H to have been human, so desperately she wished. Then she remembered how she reacted in a board meeting full of humans. Her jaw tightened.

"Yes. I hate being called Warden. I'm not a keeper, I'm not a prison guard. I'm Elif and I should be called that. I don't want to be named after a function. I was called Elif—but by who? Where did my name come from?" Parents usually gave humans their names, but she wasn't sure if this was the case for her. No one had told her anything about her family, if she even had one.

"The Interplanetary Mission designated you as the Warden of this planet. It is your title, and it is an important one."

"But I don't *want* to be called that!" she shouted, arms waving, words echoing off the smooth walls of the Garden. The watering can flew to the side of the Garden. "Even someone as stupid as Bishop has a name. Did you know his first name is Julian? That's how he signed off on the resource package dossier. *Julian Bishop*. It's a name. It sounds complete. It's... who you are. I don't have a family name. I'm just Elif."

The AI remained silent. Its metallic head swivelled downwards, as if looking at the ground.

"No one's known by their function. No human, anyway. His family wouldn't call him 'Commander Bishop'. His kids wouldn't call him that, or his friends. He'd just be Julian to them."

VAS-H moved away from Elif and roved up and down the rows of planted seeds. She watched as the AI's shell trundled around the Garden. Her face felt hot again.

"I don't want to be known as the Warden, because that's my job. But that's not—"

"Young Warden, look."

The watering can lay on top of the third batch of seeds, planted three weeks ago. A little green leaf poked out just below the spout, nearly crushed under the weight of the gardening tool. Elif moved the watering can away. The sapling bounced back to its position, sprouting three leaves. She stroked their surfaces between her fingertips, felt the delicate veins. It had taken three years since her first assignment to finally see the colour of life. Elif looked at the place card stuck into the ground in front of the plant.

"*Dahlia pinnata*," she said softly. *Asteraceae family*.

"You must be incredibly overjoyed, young Ward—"

"My name is Elif Astera. That's my whole name now, alright, Vash?" She stared at the AI shell. Green lights flickered from its voice box.

"Affirmative, young Elif."

Polaris

A small infant screamed at the top of its lungs, hidden away in their carrier. Isobel Aremu could not see whether the child was a boy or a girl, but it did not matter. Her daughter had screamed the same as a baby, and then her granddaughter after. They had both moved away, temporarily. 'Just until the media circus dies down', her daughter had said.

Leaflets were being distributed throughout the city-ship, and Isobel had kept the one that was shoved into her hand on her walk to the cafe. She unfolded its crumpled edges on the table. It was unusual that this campaign had taken to print media. Protests were usually found via media channels across the ship's intranet, and these were easier to control and monitor. The Ministry of Legislation was swift to act on anyone hacking the central network to force the uninhibited dissemination of protest information. But physical materials, like these leaflets, the banners, the marches across the plaza? This was unprecedented.

INTERPLANETARY MISSION COMPLICIT
IN ABUSE OF A MINOR

Multiple credible reports confirm the existence of an unaccompanied minor on Maoira-I, a previous planet of interest. According to internal sources, the Maiora-I project was shut down 14 years ago due to the failure of the first crewed mission. Then why has the Mission authorised a child to reside alone on a planet with no other humans? We must have answers. We must act now. We must not let these criminals get away with the abuse of the most vulnerable in our society.

A logo of gold foil flickered at the bottom right corner: a simple illustration of Old Earth with two lines shooting off from the planet. The Return to Earth Collective. A thorn in the side of her career since before she made Commander, the Collective had now shifted its focus on this fresh piece of news. At least with their primary protest—the dissolution of the Mission and to return to humanity's home planet—she could call on her contacts in the media, persuade them to amplify the Mission's cause over their noise. It was easy to shift the tide when public opinion polls showed that the majority of fleet residents (though a dwindling majority) would prefer to remain in the capable hands of the Mission. But this was different. This was playing on people's emotions, not about some far-off notion of the past. Emotions were always difficult to manage.

A green vine lingered near Isobel's shoulder. She pushed it away, watched as the leaves shivered at her touch. They must be real, not like the artificial kind in most establishments. It would explain why the cafe felt humid, why it did not have the generic cool that much of Polaris maintained. She followed the vines to the ceiling as they spread out like a spider's web across the rest of the busy cafe. String lights were threaded throughout the plants, warm, soft lights that brought an ambient glow, an almost nostalgic warmth. Isobel drank her coffee, settling into her seat. Of all the city-ships, Isobel loved Polaris the most. Her entire life was intertwined in its recesses like the vines on the ceiling.

A pale hand appeared on top of the chair opposite her.

"You're late."

"My apologies." Julian Bishop sat down and glanced around at the cafe. "It's a little difficult to get away from the office. You know, after dealing with your departure."

She knew he was relishing the fact that he no longer had to call her Commander. That title was now his. If that was all he wanted, then so be it.

"Julian, you called this meeting."

"I didn't think you'd be too busy, unless you were spending retirement taking up another job?"

A waiter came over, ready for their order.

"Just a coffee for me, thanks." Julian turned to Isobel. "Anything for you? My treat."

She would not give him the pleasure of treating her like his grandmother. Isobel glanced back at the young girl and nodded a polite dismissal.

"All good. Now, Julian, why am I here?"

Julian Bishop scratched the base of his neck. He was not wearing his uniform, just a simple sweater and slacks, but his posture belied his background, as if a metal rod was hammered through his spine.

"She's proving to be problematic." His words were strained yet quiet, as if admitting the difficulty of a task was out of his nature. "Refuses contact after the last disastrous meeting."

Isobel barked a laugh. "With the board? I'm not surprised. She's just a child." He was a decade her junior but she was sure a couple of fresh wrinkle lines had appeared on his forehead. "And she's your problem now, seeing as you wanted the job so badly."

Another waiter placed a steaming mug of coffee on the table. Julian glared the young man off before taking a gulp of the hot liquid without so much as a wince.

"Someone has to clean up your mess," he spat.

"If I recall correctly, this was your mess to begin with," said Isobel calmly. "You cannot expect her to behave like an adult."

"If she doesn't want to contact us, then so be it. It's her funeral."

Isobel sharply glanced around the cafe; no one was paying attention to their conversation. The mother with the screaming baby had already left and it was quieter. She weighed her words carefully.

"Perhaps this was the case some years ago. But now there is an apparent leak and the press won't let this go. Perhaps, even, the leak comes from the board itself."

Her successor's brow creased, his mouth a thin line.

"Impossible," he said, though she knew he didn't believe his own words.

"Have you tried telling her the truth?"

Julian scoffed. "Because you were too much of a coward to do that yourself? And don't even bother saying she's a child or she deserves to know, because that was just as true two years ago as it is now."

Isobel dropped her voice. "Because two years ago, there was a chance that Maor– that the planet was viable, that there would be a potential group joining her. Now that chance no longer exists."

She had hissed the words, as if wanting to carve them into Julian's mind. She continued, "She was never meant to be there. You know how stringent our preflight checks are for mission crews—absolutely no chance of pregnancy. We made the best we could of a bad situation. A terribly tragic situation."

"And you want me to explain this to a teenager, that she is likely to die on her own, rather than the public?" He spoke without skipping a beat.

Isobel leant back in her chair, sliding the leaflet across the table. "Don't you think it is far easier to convince one person than several millions?"

Chapter Eight

The more Elif read about Old Earth, the more she wondered about its ocean. It was ironic that a planet called 'Earth' was mostly made up of water. In the years before the Collapse, the rich blue of the seas had faded to dirty saffron. She sat in the workshop, typing lines of code into her tablet as a Vesterian documentary played on the big screen. Archival footage showed rolling tides on a sandy beach; a small stream in an emerald-green forest; the icy seas of a tundra where pure white mountains called icebergs reigned over the water.

A calm voice narrated over the footage. "The world's oceans were a vital part in the survival of humanity. Without the presence of vast bodies of water, civilisations would have crumbled before they began. 'The seven seas' was a colloquial term for the world's oceans that were divided by territory: the Indian Ocean..."

The lights in the workshop flickered. Elif looked up at the fluorescent bulbs but the flickering had already stopped. It was becoming a common occurrence. The documentary blared in the background as she crept back into the control room and brought up the atmospheric readings. It had become more than a habit to check the readings a few times a day, and each time made her stomach writhe with nerves, refusing to settle until the readings came back to normal.

"In the era leading up to the Collapse, temperatures in the ocean began to rise, a cause for concern for international climatologists. The seven seas became chambers of acidification as atmospheric CO_2 rose. In turn, the increase in acidity led to the decline of several ecosystems..."

> *Atmospheric pressure — 1001 mb*
> *Mean av. temperature — 5.8°C*
> *Wind speed — 26 mph*
> *Humidity — 71%*

Elif frowned. She ran the report again, though she knew it was pointless. The numbers wouldn't change..

"... the deepest irony is that what brought humanity life, energy and community would be the downfall of us all."

She stepped back into the workshop, one foot through the door while the other remained in the hallway. On the screen, blue oceans were replaced with footage of the interior of a fleet ship.

"We are now grateful to have such an effective filtration system, running on all five ships of the fleet. These systems were developed by Professor Aya, part of the first generation of..." The camera panned through several doors and nondescript hallways before emerging into a large, open area, like a central plaza. Hundreds of people were either walking around, chatting on benches or sitting on the ground beneath a large fountain of water. Bright lights simulated sunlight. Across the plaza, large windows showed the absolute black of space, dotted with stars.

Elif stared at the screen, watching but not really watching. Her nerves were about to reach a crescendo, and she'd need to run to the lavatory before it was too late. The computer in the control room beeped, indicating the report was over. Then a high-pitched ringing filled the room.

Atmospheric pressure — 998 mb
Mean av. temperature — 4.9°C
Wind speed — 29 mph
Humidity — 75%

LEVEL TWO ATMOSPHERIC CHANGES DETECTED

AUTOMATIC LOCKDOWN INITIATED

*

"And has this occurred before?" asked Commander Bishop.

Level Two meant leaving the Base was prohibited unless an automated mission was planned to extract personnel from the planet. Level One meant death was certain if you left the safety of the Base.

Elif shook her head. "Not since nearly twenty years ago. Back when the Base was first established, I guess." She paused. "Will this affect the engineer's arrival?" Elif still hadn't made her mind up whether she wanted a helper or not.

"We're still finalising the details of that," muttered Bishop. She nodded, watching as his focus seemed lost in a daze.

"There is some good news though," she said, as if to recapture his attention.

He blinked at her, pale eyes still as unpleasant as the day she met him. "Oh?"

"There has been confirmative plant growth in the Garden." Her voice trembled as she said it, words unsure of themselves. The Commander nodded, but she could tell he wasn't really listening. His mind was elsewhere. Her biggest breakthrough was simply a footnote in a larger conversation. *I knew I shouldn't have started with the weather changes.*

"We were aware of the seasonal changes of the planet long before you were placed on it."

Elif frowned. "How?"

He waved a hand. "From our preliminary findings. We just didn't realise how drastically they'd change. Still, it would be a good idea to see how you fare in such weather."

"You want me to stick out the storm? What if it destroys the Base? What if I d– what if conditions are unlivable?"

"Nonsense, Warden," said Bishop. Elif gritted her teeth, the title grating on her already frayed nerves. "Our Bases are designed to withstand the toughest of environmental changes. They're made by our best engineers, the same people who keep the fleet in such good shape."

"But those people haven't lived on a planet. They haven't lived on *this* planet. They don't know it as well as I do," she said despite herself. "They don't know how big this storm is going to get."

Bishop looked directly at the camera, his gaze piercing through the grainy transmission. Elif shrunk in her seat.

"Warden. You would do well to remember your place."

Elif gripped the edge of her seat, her jaw set. Then she stood up.

"No, *you* should remember *my* place. *I'm* the Warden of this planet, not you. I know this place better than... than... better than you know how to run the Mission!" Her eyes widened as soon as the words left her mouth.

A smirk grew across the Commander's face.

"I see your confidence has grown since the last meeting. Which, might I remind you, leaving without reason is a breach in your contract as Warden."

"What contract?" she spat, though she wanted to ask what exactly *was* a contract.

"The one your parents signed off before you were born. Well, 'parents' is a strange word. The woman who carried you for nine months, then birthed you. Then gave you away." He seemed to relish in the words he spoke, slowly emphasising each one. "A breach in contract means taking away certain privileges."

"Like what?"

"You mean you want to find out?"

Being threatened was a new experience. Elif's legs turned to warm jelly. She sat back down again.

"No. I don't."

*

Elif didn't feel like a warden.

"*A warden is someone who is in charge of or cares for or has custody over persons, animals or things,*" she recited, "*or, the highest executive officer in charge of a prison.*" She sat on the floor of the outer airlock, tablet connected to the inside of the Transporter with two wires. "I don't really feel like I'm 'in charge' of anything though."

"You are still the caretaker of the Base," came VAS-H's voice.

"Am I really?" she said absently, typing away at the tablet's screen. "Seems like you do all the hard work. I'm just here to watch and wait. I don't even know what I'm waiting for."

The wind speed had picked up since her conversation with Bishop the previous day. Elif didn't dare leave the confines of the Base. The wind scraped at the walls and roof of the Base, like an animal that was fighting to be let in, and she hated it. No, it wasn't hate. It was something far more visceral, an instinct she fought to ignore but would soon overwhelm her. Fear.

The sky darkened in the airlock windows. Loose dust whipped up from the ground into frenzied funnels. This world was waking from its ghostly slumber into a fitful rage. Was the planet itself alive? It was a ridiculous question—it was no more alive than VAS-H was—but as she listened to the screams of the wind, she wondered if the land was trying to tell her something.

"Alright, I've uploaded the encasement code into the Transporter." She got up from the floor and plugged the vehicle into the airlock's outlet. "You should be able to find your way into it now. It'll help you stabilise within the Transporter's circuits. You ready?"

"Affirmative."

She pressed a few commands on her tablet. A faint echo came from within the vehicle. Elif swung herself into the Transporter's seat. The echo became a murmur, but still not clear. She muttered to herself for a few minutes as she changed some more configurations on her tablet. A bold green light switched on next to the small black screen, its normal use to tell the driver if the vehicle had enough charge.

"VAS-H, you there?"

"Define 'there'."

Elif smirked. "You can hear me inside the Transporter, correct?"

"Correct."

"Great," said Elif, "now try the main controls."

Without warning, the Transporter lurched forwards before braking immediately just in front of the outer door. The vehicle then reversed just as sharply, jolting an unbuckled Elif into the wheel.

"Watch it, you're going to kill me!"

The vehicle braked just before the inner door.

"There is not a lot of room to test the controls," said VAS-H.

The AI's voice sounded tinny, almost small and withered. There was a chance this wouldn't work, that VAS-H's outdated software would buckle under the pressure of being stretched out too far from the Base. But Elif wasn't sure how long the storm was going to last, and it was safer to send the AI out than herself. Besides, if there was any danger, VAS-H would pull the Transporter back home.

"We'll have to try it outside. Let me get off first." Elif opened the door as a bright flash lit up the airlock. For less than a second, her vision flooded with pure white. She jumped back into the Transporter. A crack reverberated across the sky, a colossal sound that left the air shivering. She clutched her tablet tight and shut her eyes, listening to the tremble of her breath. What was happening? Another tremendous crack whipped through the air, like the sky itself had split and its fragments were falling to the ground. Then there was silence. Not even the wind scratched at the walls.

"What was that?" breathed Elif.

"Please specify." VAS-H's voice sounded further away than usual.

"What was that light? And that loud crash?"

"The first is lightning, the second thunder. Both common meteorological phenomena that occur during periods of low atmospheric pressure."

Of course it was thunder and lightning. How could she have been so naive, so childish? Still, her heart hammered against her chest. Her legs and arms felt numb. She didn't want to move.

Another strange sound filled the air. Elif's body tensed in fear once more, but this sound was different, not unlike the fall of water when she took a shower. Only it felt more whole, more purposeful. More real. She poked her head out of the Transporter, gingerly eyeing the airlock's window.

It was rain.

Interlude I

I turned sixteen today, the same day I learned there is no one else coming to this planet. Bishop told me this morning. It was the first time in a year since the storms began that the Mission was able to connect to me. Bishop said it was too dangerous to risk another life when the planet's weather was so unstable. I said that I was alive and well here and that the storms were beginning to settle down. He ignored me. Thankfully there was someone sensible amongst the Mission officials who acknowledged my previous weather predictions. A year ago, they sent ahead for triple the amount of resources. I've had to ration it all out.

I had climate projections ready to report to Bishop but he wasn't interested. He said they would be in contact in due course for the next plan of action, but that's all the Mission ever says.

Part of me wonders if 'Polaris' even exists, or any of the others in the fleet: Vesteris, Mathilas, Khazini, Borealis. What if it's just Bishop and some other people living on the other side of this world, just pretending to be from outer space?

I've sent VAS-H further afield in the Transporter. The storms are just as bad as they have been for the past year, but there's a slight change. The soil is softer, retaining moisture far more easily. In the collected sample, some seed-like material was scattered but they were broken pieces, really. Nothing germinated, no sign of life. Even the trees are still dead.

Later on, I asked VAS-H if the Mission would let me die all on my own. VAS-H maintained I wasn't on my own, that I had it for company. Then it sent me to the infirmary for a psychological health check. Maybe it was because I mentioned the word 'die'.

But why was I even looking forward to another person coming to this planet? The only people I know are Aremu, Bishop and the people in documentaries and films. I don't really like any of them. And I don't want other humans to come to Maoira-I. I don't need anyone else. I've managed sixteen years without a single soul except me and VAS-H. We don't need any of them.

END OF LOG

MISSION LOG Maoira-I
MISSION 4B
Log 821:

When the storms first began, I used to hide in my bed. I didn't mind the rain, that was soothing. I like listening to it as I walk to and from the Garden, as I fix the Transporter, as I eat my three meals a day, as I watch another show. But when the winds pick up and the skies darken, I'd go back into my bunk and hide under the covers. Thunder is too loud, lightning too sudden. I don't like either. I can't stay under the covers forever though, and these storms don't let up easily. So during the day I blast music throughout all the rooms of the Base, as loud as I can. VAS-H tells me I need to be careful. Apparently loud music is not good for my auditory health. I play it anyway.

I haven't heard from Bishop since a few months now, probably because they can't connect to me through the erratic weather. Not having heard from anyone means not knowing when, or if, the next package of resources will be coming. Not knowing that means I have to ration my food more strictly. I don't like that idea, but I don't have a choice. I went to the kitchen and brought out everything that was stocked in the cupboards and cold containers and listed it all out, including the mandatory vitamins. How can something be mandatory if you run out of it?

Counting everything out makes me scared. I've always known another package would arrive on schedule each month, but even if it did, how would I retrieve it? What if it's blown away or destroyed by the storm? What if it doesn't even make it through the upper atmosphere?

I hate feeling scared. It makes my thoughts fuzzy and my face feels warm and I want to cry. But I can't do anything if I just cry. Crying won't solve the problem in front of me. It won't give me food.

END OF LOG

MISSION LOG Maoira-I
MISSION 4B
Log 905:

There are calm days and stormy days. On the calm days, it rains. I send VAS-H out on days like this, loading its software into the Transporter before I keep myself safe inside the workshop. I watch as the Transporter rolls itself out of the airlock, knowing I would suffocate in the air that fills that space. It's strange, standing a few centimetres away from certain death.

VAS-H had taken some more soil samples. When I unloaded the rack from the bottom of the vehicle, it was stuck. Something had jammed the rack inside the loading mechanism. It took a few tries to pull it out, but once I did I was covered in dirt. Not just dirt though. Little green plants too.

END OF LOG

MISSION LOG Maoira-I
MISSION 4B
Log 1032:

The vitamins have run out. I always knew it was going to happen, but now it has I'm scared again. I need them to stay healthy because food alone doesn't have all the nutrients I need, even the vegetables I'm growing. And once they run out, what do I do then? I don't want to get sick. Last time I had a fever I didn't get out of bed for a couple of days. VAS-H brought me some pills and a heat pack from the infirmary when I didn't have the energy to get my head off the pillow. And that was just from a cold. What happens if I catch something more serious?

END OF LOG

MISSION LOG Maoira-I
MISSION 4B
Log 1121:

After five and a half years, the atmosphere has returned to a safe level. When I first ventured outside in the biosuit, I was blinded by pure white. I panicked as I thought it was lightning again, this time striking me as I was outside. I hate the way panic rises up inside me like a strong wave that I can't stop. Even after the stimulus is gone, my nerves still itch from within.

The bright light was sunlight. Pure sunlight from the twin suns. The sky is no longer shrouded in several layers of clouds. The sky is a creature in itself. It runs vast and boundless and is a painting of so many vivid shades: lavender and periwinkle and violet, strokes of bright orange and red at sunrise and sunset, deeper blues in the evening. It's nothing like it was years ago, when this world was dead.

The biosuit was unnecessary. Its own readings indicated safe oxygen and CO_2 levels. The crisp air settles in my lungs like a new blanket, cool yet fresh. It makes me want to breathe more, to gulp the air and drink it and let it wash my insides. Now I want to spend as much time as I can outside.

The soil is soft and responsive. I've left a trail of footprints wherever I walk. When touched, it is moist and cool. Further away from the Base, the ground is brushed in green. There are small plants growing everywhere. The dead tree trunks are still dead, and disintegrating slowly, but their bark is covered in carpets of green. Tree saplings grow amongst the trunks, their roots deeper than their branches. They will be towering trees soon enough.

I planted the seeds from the Mission into this new ground, each small mound just beyond the shadow of the Base. VAS-H is now on its first expedition of the season, a couple miles south.

I've considered naming the seasons. I can't account for the time when I was too young to be permitted outside the Base, but the first one I lived through was the dead season. It felt hollowing, as if the world wanted to seep into my veins and force me to curl inside myself to rest. Perhaps the world wanted to rest too.

And yet now, when I see the twin sunrise, when I can finally see the stars glisten in the night sky and watch this world's three moons wink at me, I wonder how I could ever go back inside the Base. How can I sleep in there when there's so much to see around me? I've never felt smaller and more insignificant than when I lie on the ground and look up, and yet there is a warm sensation that overtakes me. As if I am safe, and that I belong. That I am home.

END OF LOG

MISSION LOG Maoira-I
MISSION 4B
Log 1354:

Every month I set aside a day to run maintenance on VAS-H. I power the main processing unit down, which I can do from the control panel. I don't need to go into the core processor room, which is hard to access, because it's dark and cramped. I feel like I'm blind and trapped in there. I've only been inside once, to see what it looked like, and then I ran out.

Sometimes I'll leave VAS-H off for a while as I go for a walk, wandering as far as my legs will take me. I know it's risky because anything could happen out here. The AI wouldn't be able to notify the Mission of my status. Though what good could they do, millions of miles away from me? But I walk regardless of all this because I know I'll be safe. I've walked these paths hundreds of times before, ingrained in my mind like indelible ink.

I'll sit on a hill, moist and green and teeming with taller plants, and listen to the chitterings of small creatures, watch as pearlescent clouds touch the peaks of mountains in the distance before disappearing into nothingness. Beyond the hill, where there used to be a plain, patches of green grow like crystals across ice. The tree saplings are beginning to show their height, their branches and trunks slightly thicker and coarser, their leaves already as large as my hands. It will take time before they even resemble their ancestors. I wonder if they will grow any vegetation native to this land.

From what I've watched and read, wherever you find one human, there will always be another. And another. And another. We are like an infection that replicates itself until the host organism is completely overrun, unable to get rid of the disease.

Old Earth before the Collapse was a beautiful place too. I see the humans that are associated with the Collapse files and it's obvious why it happened in the first place, maddeningly obvious that it makes me feel sad inside. Not the hollow sadness that came with living on a barren, dry wasteland, but a deep sorrow that reaches out to the past and tries to grab hold of it before it disappears.

END OF LOG

MISSION LOG Maoira-I
MISSION 4B
Log 1398:

Music no longer has a strong pull on me. It sounds like noise, pointless noise that puts me on edge. I don't play it all the time like I used to. I prefer to listen to the patter of light rain, or to the wind brushing gently against the walls. I've seen movement for the first time: the small creatures that chitter during the day, no bigger than my hands, no taller than my ankles. They have grey fur and large teeth with beady eyes. I am not sure of their identity, not sure of what similar things existed on Old Earth. I'll read about it tonight. Perhaps I've discovered a new species. Regardless of this, I'm no longer the only living thing here. I'm simply a visitor of sorts, not truly native. I am the beginning of the infection, but I can stop it.

The land is fluttering its eyes open to sunlight. It knows it is time to rise. So I do too; I rise with the suns and walk around this newly green land, brushing my hands against large waxy leaves and fibrous stalks. The soil is so soft I could sleep on top of it. I should do that one day, but I feel tired often. I can't walk longer than a mile, even if I push myself.

I've examined the contents of this new soil. There is so much moisture retained it's hard to believe this is the same dry soil from years past. Even the air itself holds a different humidity; instead of trapping heat like an oven, it casts a soft blanket over the land, covering its inhabitants in pleasant warmth.

END OF LOG

MISSION Log Maoira-I
MISSION 4B
Log 1411:

New protocols for any planetside AI are sent directly to the database from the Mission. We are told to periodically send updates regarding the AI back to them, so they're aware of any system faults and to ensure our own maintenance code is appropriate. It's our responsibility to keep the functions of the AI running smoothly, which means to ensure the AI is following directives. But VAS-H's external shell is no longer useful, and I wish the Mission would send a replacement. I can update the software myself but I cannot build a new shell.

Without an AI at Base, the Warden is at risk of not recognising basic safety parameters and, essentially, dying on a planet without being able to send for help. But I wonder what kind of help we are promised. If I were truly in danger and VAS-H sent out a distress signal, the Mission would receive it within twenty-four hours. Vidlinks are run on the Mission's processors, which means they are able

to transmit almost instantaneously. A distress signal is
sent from the Base station, whose hardware isn't really
at optimal conditions. In a nutshell, I would be long dead
before any help from the fleet could arrive.

END OF LOG

MISSION Log Maoira-I
MISSION 4B
Log 1413:

My eyes get fuzzy when I'm staring at screens. It hurts
so I try not to stare at them for too long. I can't write very
long logs because then I get a headache. I want to spend
more time outside, where I can stretch my limbs properly,
where my eyes can rest, where I can breathe air that is
as refreshing as a cool glass of water after a long day.
But my body aches now, not with fatigue, but possibly an
illness. I can only hope it passes soon.

END OF LOG

MISSION LOG Maoira-I
MISSION 4B
Log 1415:

Bishop makes contact once every six months. A brief call,
nothing like what Assignment Day used to be. Just a short
update on my status and the climate. There are no longer

any assignments. Perhaps he has accepted my death. I wonder if I have too.

For all my emphasis on the stability of the atmosphere, he disregards it. But he asked me something strange yesterday. It caught me off guard.

"Do you want an extraction crew to bring you home?"

In all my twenty-one years, no one has ever asked whether I wanted to go home.

I still wonder if I gave the wrong answer.

END OF LOG

Part Two

Chapter Nine

The ship screamed at Rokeya. Something was wrong.

The door to the stasis chamber was cracked open, exposing the upper half of her body. It wasn't meant to open like that. Rokeya took a deep breath before a coughing fit overwhelmed her. The air tasted strange and bitter, traces of burnt metal that scratched at her throat. Her right arm throbbed, as did her head. The bright lights were disorienting as Rokeya clambered out of the chamber. The narrow corridor spun in her eyes. Her legs buckled immediately and she fell to the floor. She shut her eyes tight before forcing herself to stand up. Two steps later she fell again, palms scraping on broken glass.

It was a stupid ship to take, already falling apart, but it was the only one Isaac wouldn't miss. She staggered to the cockpit as the pain in her arm became sharper, more focused. Rokeya looked down to see a shard of glass the size of her hand had pierced her biosuit and was stuck in her arm. It probably came from the chamber's lid. The adrenaline was keeping the full force of the pain at bay, but that wouldn't last long. Rokeya growled but didn't dare pull out the glass from her arm. It was the only thing keeping her from bleeding out.

The windshields in the cockpit were shattered. The air was thick with smoke, the smell of burning metal stronger.

Rokeya checked the readings on her left wrist, a small screen lighting up at her touch. The atmosphere was breathable, safe to remove her helmet. She slid the bulky thing off and peeled off the comms cap, her short hair slick with sweat against her head. Rokeya pulled the lever on the hatch door, a familiar hiss following as its seal decompressed. She stepped out on to the ground of this new world and took a deep breath.

The soil was soft, depressing beneath her feet like the sponge of a cake. Rokeya straightened up and placed her good hand on the hull of the ship, breathing in sharply to wash away the burning stench. But the outside air was no better; now there were too many smells that overwhelmed her, rife with the pungent scents of vegetation. A wave of nausea rippled through her so she sat on the ground. The soil had a smell too, but it cut through the acid of nausea like a clean knife. Rokeya leaned against the underside of the ship. It was heavier to stand on this world, heavier to simply breathe. The gravity was a fraction higher than that of Polaris. But sitting wouldn't do her any good. She had to keep moving.

A forest of green leaves surrounded her, fluttering gently in the warm night breeze. Most extended from branches and trunks and bushes, others were crushed beneath the weight of the crashed ship. The leaves were of all sizes: some twice the size of her head, others as long as her thumb that sprouted from thin stems and fanned out. A light film covered the larger leaves that gleamed in the ship's lights. The trees were not the giants of Old Earth; the tallest in her vicinity was barely a head above her.

Still, this juvenile forest should not have been here. Rokeya stepped towards the leaves and brushed their waxy surfaces between a thumb and finger. The last recorded climate data she could access was an arid land with no hope of plant growth. But then again, the higher-ups at the Mission were not known for their transparency. Everything was covered in layers of secrecy and darkness, including Commander Aremu's sudden departure. Rokeya did not know who had replaced the esteemed woman.

Even the families of the crew of Maoira-I were never allowed to fully grieve, refused access to the detailed information of the mission. They never knew whether their beloveds were alive or not because the press release was simple—*communication has been lost*. Rokeya knew what that meant though. They had all died.

A rush of water echoed from within the forest. The heat of this strange world seeped past the layers of her biosuit and on her skin. She wiped the sweat from her face. The pain in her arm throbbed as if it could scream; she needed medication, and fast. The ship still had its medical supplies, so she locked her helmet back on to save herself from its fumes and stepped back inside. The smoke had cleared. The control panel in the cockpit blinked at Rokeya, trying to get her attention.

The radio's butchered, she thought, *but maybe I can fix it.*

It was known within whispers at the Mission itself that communications were being sent back and forth between the Base and the fleet. That meant at least one from the original crew *must* have survived. It had been twenty-one years since the original mission. It wasn't impossible.

A few years ago, she was told that Maoira-I needed another crewmate, and that would be her. But the job was pulled from under her feet, citing 'inadequate funding'. Isaac told her it was in favour of another planet. Ever since he was promoted out of the engineering bay, Isaac Jimoh had the inside track.

He'd sit in meetings with high-level staff, the top of the top of the Mission, and yet had told Rokeya nothing in exchange for their decades-old friendship. He needed to keep his job, if only to pay for his wedding. But every now and then Isaac would let things slip, let small pieces of information drip out during lunch breaks in the canteen. He knew Rokeya, knew her family. Knew their history.

Past the broken stasis chamber was the medical supply box. Rokeya sat on the floor and opened the box with one hand, considering the options in front of her. Her fingers grazed the box of morphine tablets. It had been a while since she'd needed those.

It was not the first time Rokeya had visited a planet. She'd visited others on brief jobs as part of the set-up crew, to establish a Base within a few short months before returning back to Polaris. The fleet of five city-ships was the floating remnants of the human race—at least, those that decided not to stay on Old Earth. But humanity was not meant to remain suspended in space. Their central government had made it their first priority to find a new planet to populate and save the human race. It was a noble cause. It didn't last very long.

"Wouldn't exploring all the potential planets make more sense?" Rokeya had asked Isaac over lunch in the staff canteen. "We've got the resources to do that."

"It would," said Isaac. He wiped a small splatter of tomato soup from the edge of his beard with the back of his hand. "And that's why *you're* not in charge of deciding what happens."

*

Repairing a radio with one hand proved to be more difficult than she anticipated. Rokeya sat back in the cockpit chair and wiped her brow once again. Each movement felt heavier than the last. She had to figure out how to stay alive and not bleed to death. She'd passed over the box of morphine tablets—she'd need a clear head to navigate the next few hours, or days—and went with high-strength codeine. It barely took the edge off. She slid off the chair and slipped beneath the control panel, the overhang providing a small shelter.

The job was pulled from her over five years ago. In those years, Rokeya had researched Maoira-I as much as her security clearance would allow her. A world of ever-changing climate, lifeless deserts that morphed into destructive monsoons. In comparison to the other potential planets, Maoira-I was undesirable. A last resort, a 'maybe'. In a vast galaxy with numerous planets, it was now the lowest priority for the Mission. As her mind slipped towards her throbbing arm, Rokeya took a deep breath to steady herself. She was here for one reason, and it wasn't to save the human race.

Chapter Ten

Night on Maoira-I was nothing like Damson, Rokeya's home neighbourhood. The stone streets of Damson were lined with leafy trees and small lights at foot level that would glow brighter whenever you walked nearby. Unless you were asleep at home, Polaris was never silent. The food district just off Markaz Aya had rows of cafes and restaurants and opened out on to a viewing deck that overlooked Sabuja, the first planet that the Mission attempted to investigate. As a child, Rokeya had sat on the deck with her grandfather, her Nanabhai, listening to him tell her stories about his work. She didn't understand his work, not back then, but she loved when he took her out for ice cream and donuts, sometimes both on the same day.

On Maoira-I, the night was a shroud of silence, deep and impermeable. Rokeya nursed her arm in an awkward position on the cockpit chair. She'd removed the glass shard and bandaged her arm, though some blood had already seeped through. It needed stitching up but she'd have to figure that out later, after getting some sleep. In her good hand, Rokeya gripped the bloodied piece of glass. Just in case.

She pushed back thoughts of Isaac lecturing her about destroying one of his ships. She'd pay him back, she'd say, and he'd retort that on her wage he'd still be waiting to be paid back in the morgue. Instead Rokeya focused on the donuts Nanabhai would buy her. They were always freshly made, soft and buttery, with a sweet yellow coating and coloured sprinkles. Nanabhai knew the owner of the dessert shop so he'd get a cup of coffee on the house. He always said no, always pushed back, but couldn't refuse once the owner had forced the steaming cup into his hand. Rokeya's small hand would slip back into his on their walk to the viewing deck until she was completely taken in by the view of Sabuja. The green planet was visible through giant floor-to-ceiling windows, the only place on Polaris where the exterior hull had been replaced with layers of fused-silica glass. Sabuja and its vast oceans of copper chloride, a resource that Polaris could not make use of, hung like an emerald jewel in the black sky, untouchable.

A loud crash startled Rokeya from her dream. She jumped up, wincing at the pain that screamed in her arm, and held the piece of glass out in front of her. A blinding bright light shone through the broken windows. Rokeya dropped down to the floor and hid beneath the control panel, heart pounding against her chest.

Get it together, idiot.

Several smaller knocks came from the hull. Was someone knocking on the ship? No, that couldn't be it. It sounded like when the hatch door would jam in its own mechanism and constantly slam into the groove. Rokeya took a deep breath and got up.

She gripped the handlebars of the steps tightly, lowering herself to the soft soil. Nothing moved in the dark. There was no other sound except the whirring of wheels and a faint squeaking at the front end of the ship. She crept round, good hand shaking as she held the glass shard out.

Jammed into the ship's broken hull was a machine twice as tall as Rokeya. Wide headlamps shone into her ship's windshields. Large wheels were stuck in the pit of dirt the ship had created. Rokeya froze for a few moments before shaking herself out of it. This vehicle was manmade, so it must be something she could use. Beneath layers of dirt on the machine's surface was a smudge of red. As Rokeya came closer, she saw the old logo of the Interplanetary Mission, the logo used when the fleet first launched hundreds of years ago. Two circles looping over each other, a seven-pointed star within them.

"Hello?" she called out to the driver. "Are you stuck?"

She placed the glass inside a pocket and climbed on to the vehicle's steps, pulling herself up by a handlebar. Through the dusty windows, the vehicle appeared unmanned.

That's odd. I'm sure this class is made to be driven.

Rokeya opened the door and thrust herself inside. It was an older model, something even Isaac probably wouldn't know how to fix unless someone gave him a manual. A bold green light shone beside its black screen. It had enough battery.

"Alright, let's steer you out of here." With one hand, Rokeya attempted to reverse the vehicle. The lever was jammed in position. She pressed on the black touchscreen, expecting to see a menu, but nothing happened. The vehicle would not respond to her command. "What's wrong with you?"

"I appear to be stuck."

Rokeya shrieked, jumping up.

"The wheels are turning but the Transporter is not moving."

Rokeya backed out without looking and fell out of the open door. The soft soil cushioned her landing.

Did it just... talk?

"There seems to be something blocking the path. It cannot be manoeuvred around." A flat voice resounded overhead, neither male nor female. It spoke with purpose.

"Are you talking to me?" whispered Rokeya as she poked her head back in through the door.

"Yes, I am. Are you here to help me?"

The piece of glass was hidden in Rokeya's suit, but there was no way she could use it. How would you even attack a disembodied voice?

"I—yeah, sure. I can help you." She peered over the windshield. "Can you dim the lights? It's too bright for me to see."

The owner of the voice obliged.

"Great, now put yourself into reverse." Rokeya dropped outside. She pushed on the vehicle's front with her good shoulder, trying to shove it out of the ditch as the wheels turned backwards. After a few moments, the vehicle broke free, driving away into the darkness. Rokeya stared as the lights dimmed in distance, hanging like watchful eyes in the shadows between trees.

Then the headlamps blinked twice, beckoning her to follow.

Chapter Eleven

Rokeya didn't sit inside the vehicle again. It felt intrusive, so she contented herself to walk beside it. Its wheels rolled heavily across the forest floor, crushing foliage beneath synth-rubber tyres. Its headlamps cast a wide net of light across the path ahead. They walked towards a dark gap in between the trees, a gap that grew steadily larger. The hum and echo of animals skittered through the forest's air.

Stars scattered across smoky white wisps in the dark sky. But Rokeya couldn't look up for too long, as nausea came in slow waves followed by bouts of dizziness. She held on to a handlebar to steady herself. Polaris was somewhere amongst those stars. Her parents lived on the city-ship of Khazini, had moved there when the hustle and bustle of the capital became too much.

There, at the bottom of the hill, was a Mission Base Station. Rokeya knew the rigid architecture, had briefly lived in one herself, had helped build newer models for various other planets of interest. It was a squat, rectangular shape with antennas poking out of the solar-panelled roof. But the silence of the Base was too loud as she came down the hill, gripping the vehicle's handlebar on the slope. The building's outside

walls were lit with thin panels of fluorescent white lights, a few
of them broken. Some cracks had spread across the walls, but
aside from that the building looked in decent shape. How had
it withstood the force of the planet's storms?

"Is there someone here?" she asked the vehicle, feeling a
little stupid as she did so. There was no reply.

On the side of the Base was the entrance to the outer
airlock. A few feet from the entrance was a square fence,
something not entirely Mission specification. Rokeya peered
over the fence to see growing vegetation, stems thick with
leaves and some bearing fruit. The plants were verdant, shining
green like small jewels from Sabuja. The hatch opened as they
approached, both machine and human walking inside, and
the room lit up. A stream of disinfectant spread over them.
Rokeya knew the procedure, but it still stung as the fine mist
snuck into the cuts and scrapes on her exposed face.

The inner door unlocked with a click, its edges illuminated.
Rokeya looked inside the vehicle—now visible in the harsh
white light, covered in layers of dirt and dust—but all its lights
were off.

She knocked on the window. "Hello?"

"Are you looking for something?" The same flat voice filled
the airlock, emanating from all angles. It *was* an AI, then,
somehow connected to the Base's vehicle. *Smart.*

Rokeya stepped back and looked around the airlock. If the
Base was still running and the AI was functional, then there
must be a human present on this planet. "I'm here to see the
crew. Or whoever has kept you running."

"Where have you come from?" asked the AI.

Rokeya paused. The AIs back on Polaris always stuck to
protocol, to ask questions only in line with their manufacturer's

directive. All the AIs installed within Base Stations were tasked with ensuring safety of the Base and habitability for a small group of humans. They measured atmospheric parameters essential for survival. They answered directly to questions and always obeyed directives.

"I'm a senior engineer from the Interplanetary Mission. I was sent here to help. You know, to reinforce the crew."

"All missions were cancelled." There was no change in inflection or tone, but the very statement felt accusatory.

"They were," admitted Rokeya, "but I wanted to help anyway. Can you direct me towards the crew quarters?" As she said it, she edged towards the inner door.

"We have received no approved instructions for an engineer."

The doorframe darkened. Without thinking, Rokeya rammed her bad shoulder against it to no effect. The pain screamed once more.

"Open this door. That's an order."

"I cannot," came the smooth voice.

"But you locked it," said Rokeya, frustration bleeding through her voice. Her arm throbbed. The dizziness took hold of her. She leant her head against the doorframe. Crimson soaked the bandage on her arm. Her entire body ached as her pulse throbbed across her body. The edges of her vision darkened. She licked her dry lips.

"Conditions for automatic override are three," she muttered. "First…"

She was sure the AI said something in response, but she had already collapsed on the floor.

Chapter Twelve

Rokeya woke up confused. Her thoughts did not match up to her senses. There was a cool, hard floor where there should have been her bed; the sharp, astringent smell of disinfectant when her apartment usually smelled of cinnamon coffee.

Then it came back to her: the crash, the injury, the insubordinate AI. Her shoulder throbbed worse than before she had collapsed.

"Need..." she muttered. "Infirm... infirmary."

Nothing happened. The lights of the airlock were blinding. Rokeya forced her thoughts to rise above the pulses of pain. What was the phrase again? There were a collection of commands that all registered AI were bound to comply with, and under no circumstances could they disobey. But Rokeya had never come across an AI that had been tampered with.

"Activate..." she groped for the words. "Activate Protocol: Infirmary." Once more, nothing happened. Rokeya pushed herself up against the door that was still locked, inhaling sharply with every movement. It was no use. She was too weak, had lost too much blood. She slumped back to the floor.

"I need help," she whispered, closing her eyes. Rokeya wondered if she would die here, all alone on a planet that nobody wanted. That nobody would ever come to.

"Help..." Her words drifted into the air as a fresh wave of agony hammered through her. "Help... mayday."

Her eyes opened slowly. The word had fallen from her lips like a feather.

"Mayday," said Rokeya, a little louder than before. "Activate Protocol: Mayday."

The lights in the airlock dimmed. An arrow flashed bright green above the door she leant against. A whoosh echoed; all the doors within the Base had opened. Rokeya steered herself against the wall and stared at the open doorway. Thick lines of light lined the floor. The doorway inside the inner airlock was just a few feet away, with yet another bright green arrow above it. It would lead to the infirmary. Rokeya lifted herself up, crying out before straightening up at the door. If the layout of this Base was the same as all the others, the infirmary was located at the centre of the building to ensure the shortest distance travelled at any point in the Base.

The corridor from the airlock cut through a control bay. Rokeya paused at the second doorway. A tattered computer chair sat in the midst of the large monitors, the black leather worn down after years of use. She held on to the doorframe, staring at the chair. She could picture him sitting there, his posture gradually curving as the hours wore on, like it always did in his workshop. He'd hear the patter of her little feet and swing around in the chair with a big smile on his wrinkly face.

The pain brought her back. Rokeya grunted as she shifted her way through the corridors. She would not die here. She still had a mission to complete.

The infirmary was brightly lit and encased behind tempered glass walls. Inside were two examination tables either side of the room, each one curved slightly upwards like a bed. A large screen was attached to each bed. The infirmary was like the one tucked away at the Mission Centre, organised yet busy, filled with cupboards of medications, emergency injections, bandages and dressings. But this place looked much older, with its bulky screens and uncomfortable beds. Rokeya rummaged through the drawers and pulled out what she needed: sterile water, gauze swabs, adhesive bandage strips. She'd get to the strong painkillers in a moment. Rokeya was an engineer, not a medic, but she was still expected to know basic first aid. Trouble was, she could never concentrate in those classes, and never had the patience to suture a fake wound properly. She hitched herself on the closest bed with the gear in a box and unravelled the bandage from her shoulder. After cleaning the dried blood away, it didn't look so bad. She could still move her hand and fingers, though with some difficulty. The bandage strips were tricky to apply, especially with one hand. Rokeya shimmied her weight on the bed; as she sat in the centre, a small beep came from the bed. The attached screen activated, switching on.

KHAN, Latif – is this the same patient?
Press Y to continue
Press N to start a new session

Rokeya froze. She slid herself closer to the screen, wincing as her open wound gaped in the cool air. She raised her good hand to the screen and selected Y.

The screen dissolved into another, showing vital signs and a patient history. The dates were over two decades ago. There was a photo in the top right corner. There he was, with his tufts of grey curls and a small, tired smile on his wrinkled face.

Nanabhai.

Chapter Thirteen

With no warning, the doors to the infirmary slid shut. Rokeya looked up, muscles tense. Was the AI disobeying orders again? She slid off the bed and crept closer to the glass doors, footsteps silent on the smooth floor. The air filtration system sputtered overhead. Rokeya had no weapons at hand, nothing to defend herself with. Standing against the glass door would be unwise, especially if it were to break. She couldn't afford another injury. On her approach, the doors slid open once more. Rokeya wilted, shoulders deflating. There was nothing wrong with the system; the AI hadn't trapped her in the infirmary. She was being paranoid for no reason.

"Close the wound, take the drugs, close the wound, take the drugs," she muttered to herself, turning back to the equipment scattered on the bed. The pain was interfering with her logic, and that was the most concerning factor. She sat back on the bed and glanced at the image of her grandfather before applying the first bandage strip with a shaky hand.

"This is all your fault. If it wasn't for you, I wouldn't be here. If you didn't have to be so good at your job, you wouldn't have been hired on the Mission and I wouldn't have tried to follow you. You were meant to stay retired."

Rokeya was not a little girl anymore, wasn't even a young woman. She'd followed her grandfather's path into engineering but opted for a different discipline instead of artificial intelligence. Her tired body had carried her through four different planets with three different gravitational pulls in just as many decades. She'd had worse injuries than the wound she currently applied a second strip to. And yet when she stared at Nanabhai's face, she was the little girl he had abandoned on Polaris to explore a new and exciting world.

The bandage strips stuck to her open flesh, their white film dissolving to leave thin black lines that pulled the wound together on both sides. It hurt, but it would have been more painful to suture herself with a shaky hand. She wrapped a clean bandage around her arm, tying it with her teeth and free hand. She'd found the cupboard of pain relief, rifling through boxes and wrappers until she found the Morph-In injections: emergency morphine shots wrapped in individual sterile auto-injectors. Once she'd jabbed her thigh through her biosuit she made her way back to the bed. It would take a few minutes for the analgesia to kick in. Exhaustion swept through her, but somehow the hard bed felt so comfortable, like the cosiest place to sleep in the entire galaxy. She lay her head down gently at the flat end, just below the screen, allowing the fatigue to roll across her muscles—

There was a young girl just beyond the glass walls. Rokeya shrieked and jumped up, smashing her head on the bottom edge of the screen. It swung back on its connection to the bed, the joints squeaking. Rokeya cried out and clutched her head with her bad arm before realising her mistake. Pain throbbed across all her limbs. The dizziness came back again. The girl was not there. The engineer staggered out of the infirmary despite herself, hand pressing against the glass walls to make her way around the entire perimeter. There was no one else there, no other sound except her haggard breathing and water rushing through pipes overhead.

"Is there still a medical emergency?" came the flat voice overhead.

"No," said Rokeya. Almost immediately, the hallways flooded with light. She blinked fiercely in the brightness as her eyes adjusted.

"Tell me, is there a human living here?" No response. "You need to answer me. It's part of your directive."

"My directive is to protect the Base and its inhabitants," said the AI.

Rokeya leaned her head against the wall of the infirmary, its smooth surface cooling her forehead. She didn't like speaking to a disembodied voice, even if she wasn't feeling sick.

"Can you download yourself into your shell? Wherever it is."

"That is not possible. My shell has expired. It lacks capacity for my current software."

That wasn't a surprise, but it irked Rokeya that the Mission hadn't sent any update by way of physical technology. She peeled herself off the wall and walked down the hallway, glancing into each room's viewing port and seeing nothing of interest. There was so much space here, so much room for several people to live and work together. And it would have been filled too, with everyone from the initial crew: Captain Osoba, Dr Bauer, Shoji Kimura, Aida Bayram and Professor Latif Khan. Each one a specialist in their field. Each one willing to live away from their families for several years for the simple question: can humanity live here?

"You still haven't answered me," Rokeya called out. She realised she was searching for the dormitories, for a nice bed she could pass out in. Perhaps there was even a nice fluffy pillow too. She slid the door open once she'd found the right room. The lights were out and did not turn on when she stepped inside; they must have been switched off for a reason. Her helmet was back in the ship, a dumb move to make, so she couldn't access its flashlight. Rokeya switched on the smaller light in her suit's left glove. A small beam of sterile white light washed over the darkness. Clothes, wires, empty canteens and dirt were strewn across the floor. Her feet crunched on something: she looked down to see the cracked screen of a tablet. As Rokeya picked it up, a groan came from the corner of the room. She jumped up, dropping the tablet to the floor, and raised her left arm to the corner. There, in the bunk, was a lump under the covers.

Rokeya's heart pounded. Sweat slicked her skin, loose hair stuck to her neck. She edged closer, every muscle in her body protesting. For a brief moment, she wondered if it could be Nanabhai, sick beneath the covers, like she had seen him once at home. If it could be him, he would be nearing ninety years old. She gently pulled back the blanket, peering into the bunk. Her hand hovered over its occupant.

A scrawny girl in the midst of a fever dream, forehead pasted in sweat, her face pale and sallow.

Chapter Fourteen

There shouldn't be a girl on this planet. No one under the age of eighteen is permitted for space exploration, no one under twenty-one for a planetary mission. Strict rules were in place for all fleet citizens; Rokeya had to wait for her eighteenth birthday before she could participate in a spacewalk with her mechanical design class. She crept back out of the dorm, careful not to make any more noise than she already had, and allowed the door to slide close before she pressed her fist on the wall.

"You told me there was no one else here," she called out.

"I said nothing of the sort," said the AI from above.

It was true, but that wasn't the point. She hadn't been *told* anything. She hadn't seen this in the files of Maoira-I before she made the rash decision to make the journey. All five members of the set-up crew were adults. The girl didn't look any older than seventeen, with hollowed cheeks and skinny limbs. How long had she been on the planet by herself, wasting away? Had the Mission been aware of this—and for how long? Was she a stowaway?

"Who is she?" said Rokeya. "And when did she arrive on the planet?"

No response. *My directive is to protect the Base and its inhabitants.*

"Are you protecting her?" she asked once more, this time softly.

"I am."

Rokeya rubbed her eyes. She needed to rest, to allow her wound to heal and her mind to catch up. That wasn't happening any time soon. She probed further as she made her way back to the infirmary.

"I can help you, but you need to be honest with me. I won't harm her; I can help you protect her. How long has she been this way for?"

"Her temperature reached 38.1^{0}C yesterday. There are no other apparent injuries. It appears to be a viral infection. She has not been administered any antipyretics. She is usually able to do that herself but has been bed bound for the past two days." A pause, a recalculation of words. "I am unable to bring her medication if she is not able to get to the infirmary. My shell—"

"That's fine," said Rokeya, though it really wasn't. "I'm here now."

*

The girl was malnourished. Her skin was dry and thin, like a delicate piece of paper. Purple veins that were meant to stand out on her wrist were nowhere to be seen. Dehydration was taking its toll.

Rokeya was no medic. She didn't know how to start an IV line or cannulate a person, and she didn't want to try, no matter how tempting. Instead she found a box of antipyretic shots for short-term use, not for a severe illness, but she had no other choice. She sat by the girl's bed and held the auto-injector in her sweaty palm, bracing herself for any reaction. The girl turned to the side when her limp body was exposed to the cool air, a soft groan escaping her dry lips. Rokeya placed the end of the auto-injector on the girl's bony thigh and pressed down on the button. She inhaled sharply, as if she was the one being injected. The girl's body tensed up, but she remained asleep. Rokeya had wheeled over a monitor from the infirmary, following her basic training, and applied the sensors to the girl's chest and back. All her vital signs seemed normal, heart rate perhaps a little lower than average, but her temperature reading flashed bright red. Almost half an hour later, the number began to fall. Rokeya slid down to the floor and leaned against the bunk, holding her head in her hands.

None of this should be happening. And even more frustrating was the AI that refused to divulge crucial information to her. Rokeya stepped back into the hallway and headed towards what she hoped was the kitchen—if not for the girl, but her own stomach.

"So," she called out as she slipped down empty hallways, "are you still not going to tell me anything about her?" She felt like a coy teenager, asking for information about her latest crush. "Considering I might be the only one able to save her life. Not even her name?"

"Her name is Elif Astera," came the response. "She is the Warden of Maoira-I."

Rokeya stopped in her tracks. The name did not sound familiar. She stared at nothing in particular and tried to force words out of her mouth. "She's the what?"

"The Warden. The person in charge of looking after Maoira-I."

Rokeya's mouth hung open. "What the hell is a warden?"

"Someone who is in charge of or cares for or has custody over persons, animals–"

"I didn't ask for the dictionary. Why is there a young girl, practically dead to the world, alone on a planet of interest?"

"She is not dead," said the AI, rather abruptly. "She is unwell."

"It's a figure of speech, but she may as well be," snapped Rokeya. "I can't believe this. Was she born here? She can't be more than sixteen or seventeen years old—"

"Elif is twenty-one years old."

"And has anyone else been here in that time?"

"No. It has only been Elif and I."

If Rokeya didn't know any better, she'd think the AI was proud of the girl—well, woman. AIs shouldn't be able to show this kind of emotion with the subtle changes in the cadence of their voice. It unnerved her, but not more than the revelation of an abandoned child.

"Who the hell authorised this? Why was a *child* permitted to live *alone* on a planet—"

"She is not alone. Elif has never been alone. She has me."

Rokeya exhaled forcefully. "Alright, you're getting too emotional for my liking. You're not meant to be attached to those in your care."

She came upon the kitchen and immediately started for the cupboards. Plenty of empty wrappers filled the ration cupboards. Not a single one was sealed.

"You're joking," murmured Rokeya as she rifled through another. "Is there no food in this place? What happened to the ration reserves? The resource packages?"

"Elif has been rationing her food for five years," came the curt reply.

"And she's run out," said Rokeya quietly. "AI, when was the last time the Mission contacted the Base?"

"My name is VAS-H, or *Vital Auxiliary Support: H-unit*. Elif often calls me 'Vash'."

"*Fine*," said Rokeya through gritted teeth. "Vash, when was the last time the Mission contacted you?"

"The most recent communication has been from Commander Bishop, approximately six months ago."

"Bishop?" said Rokeya. "Julian Bishop is the Commander now?"

"Affirmative. He has been Commander for six years."

Rokeya leant against the kitchen counter. One of the tube lights flickered, needing to be replaced. She closed her eyes.

It took me six years to get here. Her parents were older now, and she'd likely missed Isaac's wedding. He probably had at least one kid by now. He'd always wanted children. What else had changed in the time she was away? Maiora-I was the furthest planet of interest. This was why a rescue mission for the set-up crew was out of the question: the risk of over a decade of spaceflight far outweighed the probable death of half a dozen crew members.

Rokeya opened her eyes, almost with a jolt. "Vash, how old did you say Elif was?"

"Twenty-one years old. She will be twenty-two in four months."

Rokeya's throat went dry.

"Was Elif born on Maoira-I?"

A pause. "I have no record of a human birth on Maoira-I."

Chapter Fifteen

The first priority was to find water. All Base Stations were equipped with an extensive water filtration unit that ran the length of the building. Each segment of the unit had a robust mechanism to filter bacteria and toxins from recycled water in urine, rainwater and any moisture from the soil. If there was a thriving forest just outside the walls, that meant there was a water source nearby, which meant the unit's underground segment should pump water extensively from the soil. In theory. Anyone trained to live in the Base would have known that, but she wasn't sure about Elif. Since VAS-H's revelation, Rokeya wasn't sure about anything.

The potable water dispenser in the kitchen was broken. Nothing came out except a drop of muddy water after a few seconds of tight gurgling. The dispensers in the infirmary, workshop and dorm were the same. Rokeya groaned after trying them all. The filtration unit was a fiddly piece of equipment that often required several engineers to run diagnostics.

"How long has the unit been out of commission?" She'd have to start rationing the words she spoke; her mouth was gritty and sore with every hour that passed.

"The most recent problem began two days ago."

"Most recent?" Rokeya keyed a code into a door at the far end of the Base. The cramped passage housed the background machines and mechanisms, a tunnel-like room that ran both overground and under; the nervous system of the whole building. VAS-H's core processor would be here somewhere too.

"There have been several issues with the water filtration unit for the past three years. These range from blockages to circulation problems. Elif has been able to fix most of these. Of course, she has recently been too unwell to attend to any issues around the Base."

Every time Rokeya heard her name, she shuddered. The thought of a young girl, a *baby*, waddling through the halls of the Base all alone squeezed her insides.

"Diagnostics from the most recent problem show a blockage in the ground filter." The AI could locate the problem, but not fix it. That would need human hands and minds. Part of her grandfather's research was to improve this, to enhance and strengthen how AIs helped humans to problem solve.

The passage was a narrow hall, darkened except for the lights that flickered from the filtration unit machine. The unit took up most of the space, with only room for a single human to shuffle down. Engineers had to be used to working in both tight spaces and the vastness of space. Several of her classmates had dropped out due to not being able to deal with either ends of the spectrum. For the most part, Rokeya ignored her surroundings when working on a problem. She inched her way through the network of narrow hallways and switched on her wristlight. It would take around fifteen minutes to reach the ground filter. Her mind drifted to Nanabhai and how he would have managed these jobs with his stiff joints and aching back. He wasn't in perfect condition when he accepted his position on the crew. It was completely unlikely he had lived longer than ten years; there was clearly no one else here except for Elif. Where was he buried, if at all? Where was the rest of the crew?

"You knew my grandfather, right?" she asked aloud in the dark. "Latif Khan. He was part of the mission crew."

"Negative. I have only worked with Elif."

Rokeya wanted to stop in her tracks but forced herself to continue.

"That's not right," she said. "You would have been installed by a set-up crew. He came after that. You would have interacted with him loads of times."

"I have no record of any humans before I was assigned to Elif."

Rokeya frowned, squeezing through a particularly tight spot. She kept talking, if only to distract herself. "There were five members of the crew. Lucius Osoba, mission captain. Anja Bauer, physician and pilot. Actually, both Osoba and Bauer were pilots. Shoji Kimura was a specialist in geology, and Aida Bayram a biologist with a special interest in botany. Then Professor Khan, my grandfather, Latif Khan. He taught robotics and electronics at the University of Vesteris before he retired to focus on his own projects. The Mission pulled him out of retirement for this expedition."

Rokeya dipped her head beneath a particularly low pipe.

"I do not have any record of these humans in my database."

Rokeya's heart sunk. It was possible the Restoration Directive had taken place, but then VAS-H would not have extensive memories of Elif. Rokeya was here to find out what happened to her grandfather, and instead she'd found an amnesiac AI. Their family had received not a single word except that *communications have been lost*. Rokeya was only fourteen then.

"Perhaps there was another AI installed before me."

Rokeya shook her head, sidling across another few metres of beeping, flashing machinery. "Impossible. You're the only class of AI that's installed on any and all Bases. Well, there have been some upgrades since, but they're still all VAS models. And even if it was an older model, the data should transfer."

She stopped in a welcome opening in the narrow hallway, a door nestled in the alcove. Rokeya shone her wristlight on the plaque across its face: *CORE PROCESSOR UNIT*. This was where VAS-H was housed, protected far away from any tampering or weathering. She waved her hand across the ID pad. Nothing happened.

"Doesn't it recognise my bio-print?"

"You are not authorised personnel."

Rokeya frowned. "Excuse me, I practically built these—"

"Not this iteration of the Base."

Rokeya wanted to ask why there wasn't an upgrade, why had the Mission not sent an engineer crew to this world as they did with others. Why was everything in this place so old and broken?

"Because they let a kid run it," she muttered under her breath before speaking louder. "This is so messed up. Since when did the Mission have the authority to settle a *child* on a planet? By herself—and no, Vash, you don't count. You're an AI. Humans need humans."

When no reply came back, Rokeya felt guilty.

"I'm sorry," she said, the first time she had apologised to an AI. "I meant she should have had another human *along with you*. But even then, no one in their right mind would send someone younger than sixteen outside a ship, even if they were accompanied. It's irresponsible. And this, right here, is beyond that."

The ground segment was housed a floor beneath the rest of the filtration unit. Rokeya edged down a set of dark steps into a basement-type room with a huge machine in its middle. The machine was built floor to ceiling, feeding into the rest of the unit above with sensors and liquid tubes anchored into the ground. Rokeya saw the problem before her second foot touched the ground.

"The filter was switched off," she said, dropping down to the lower right side of the machine. The rest of the unit was aglow with lights and buttons except this side. The pressure on the other side must have been too high, too overwhelming for the ground segment to process. For safety, it would switch off to stop the Base's pipes bursting. After pressing a sequence of switches, the filter turned back on. Rokeya adjusted the speed, allowing for smoother control of the higher pressure that came from the soil. The unit must not have been altered to accommodate for the change in seasons.

"There, that should do it," she said, sitting back with relief. Her mouth felt like sandpaper. "Now for the long hike back for a glass of water."

Chapter Sixteen

There was no other way to rehydrate the girl without tilting her head up and drip feeding her water. To do this with one functioning arm was even more difficult. Rokeya found a box of oral syringes in the infirmary—that room was turning into a goldmine—and some expired oral rehydration sachets. It was better than nothing. She allowed Elif's head to rest on three pillows before gently opening her mouth and pipetting drops of water. Some drops rolled off her cracked lips, dribbling down her chin. It took a few tries to get the angle right. Rokeya knew in this case, this kind of severe dehydration, an IV line with saline was needed. She wasn't sure what good her oral syringe would do, barely longer than her finger. It would take days to revive the girl. Rokeya hoped it wasn't longer than this. She hoped this would work. For a moment, Rokeya's panic grew deeper in the pit of her stomach. It unnerved her, how the anxiety frayed her nerves so easily. This did not happen often, if at all. She was meant to be trained for situations like this.

Not for children that are dying in my arms. She shook the thought away. No one was going to be dying with her around. Even if the food rations were finished, there was still the small plants growing outside. Rokeya was sure they were of edible vegetation, and there must have been a Garden somewhere inside the Base. The Garden was integral for the initial tasks on new planets of interest, not just to ensure the viability of life but to test agricultural production. There would be no point setting up shop on a fancy new planet if there wasn't a way for the inhabitants to eat. She'd get to making some kind of meal soon, but for now, she needed to rest, needed a proper sleep, needed another pain shot. Her limbs ached and the pain in her shoulder began to scream once more.

On her way back from the infirmary, Rokeya passed the control room and paused by its door once more. She sat on the frayed chair and stared at the screens, some of it making sense while others needed more concentration from a more focused Rokeya. How could a child have taken all this in, have understood any of these complexities; how could a child have understood how to take care of herself?

She scrolled through documents of Elif's progress, of the results from her tasks from over a decade ago. Most of the images were of the landscape of the Maoira-I from before the storm season: a deserted world with dead trees punctuating the land, a dull sky, flat ground. It was depressing. Rokeya couldn't imagine how anyone could live here alone, let alone a child. Anger grew inside her, a flicker of a flame that began since *communications have been lost*. To save a child, it would have been worth the entire fleet travelling to Maoira-I to retrieve her. She was one of theirs.

Perhaps there would be something in the Base's files about her grandfather. But after forty minutes of endless scrolling within the computer, Rokeya gave up. It was as if his existence on the planet, on this mission, had never occurred. As if he had been erased from all except her own memory. She sat back in the chair, furiously rubbing both eyes with her palms before dragging her hands down her cheeks. She kicked the desk in frustration. A drawer slid open. She peered inside, seeing a thick silver ring with an amber gem.

Rokeya was a child again, fiddling with her grandfather's ring on his finger when he'd fallen asleep on their sofa. It slid off his finger and fell into her small hand, the gem glinting in the dim living room lights. She'd placed it on her own tiny finger but it was far too big. It fell to the floor. Before she could pick it up, she was startled by a deep chuckle.

"We'll need to get you one for yourself," Nanabhai had said, a yawn on the edges of his words. "Would you like a ring, Rokeya?"

She'd nodded vigorously, the bunches of her hair bouncing in time. "Yes, yes please!"

Nanabhai chuckled again and drew her to his lap. "You see this jewel? It's a special one."

"Why?" she asked, the perennial question on a child's lips.

"It's from Old Earth. It's called amber and it comes from trees. This is a little piece of Earth. My own grandfather gave it to me, and his before him. I'll give it to you one day too."

"Why can't I have it now?" she'd whined, the threat of a tantrum forming. But Nanabhai had laughed out loud, hearty and strong, and lifted her up as he rose from the sofa.

"Why, your fingers are far too small! You're a little girl now Rokeya, but I'll give you this ring when you grow big and strong."

Back in the control room, an older Rokeya put the ring on. Tears streamed down her smiling cheeks as she watched the ring hang loose on her slim finger.

Interlude II

MISSION LOG Maoira-I
MISSION 4A
AUTHOR A.B.
Log 04:

Day 2 on Maoira-I. All mission crew have responded positively to medical testing, including myself, Dr Anja Bauer. I have some concerns about Prof. Khan, which I had voiced during pre-mission briefings. He is much older than the rest of us, and while he is mostly fit and healthy for someone of his age, his bones have weakened further during spaceflight. I have instructed him to increase his intake of calcium and vitamin D supplements and to increase his daily exercise sessions. No one will wither away here on my watch.

END OF LOG

MISSION LOG Maoira-I
MISSION 4A
AUTHOR A.B.
Log 10:

Day 7 on Maoira-I. It has been a week since we landed. The Base was established around six years ago. As with all planets of interest, an initial crew was sent to build the Mission Base Station within 3 months. I would not want to have been part of that crew. A 12-year round trip for simply 3 months? But I suppose the Mission has wasted more money elsewhere.

Maiora-I seems promising. At night, its sky is the colour of blueberry custard. There is abundant vegetation, though we have yet to see if any of these are edible for humans. There are native animals too, small creatures that roam around the dense forest nearby. They seem to have been disturbed by our arrival. Indeed, who would not be?

The trees are large, towering things with crooked shapes. Myself and Bayram went exploring in the morning, taking samples here and there. Well, her more than me. This is her field, after all. She was particularly interested in the tree bark, scraping several samples from different areas. She tells me more about her family on Vesteris, about her husband and how he protested to such a long mission. I cannot say I was met with the same protests from my family, but I only have my aging mother and I feel she wants to get rid of me as much as I her.

END OF LOG

MISSION LOG Maoira-I
MISSION 4A
AUTHOR A.B.
Log 21:

Kimura spends much of his time in the Garden. I think he is a little homesick. This is his first mission, and he is our youngest. Often times the younger crew members show more enthusiasm to take on the gruelling tasks. Not Shoji Kimura. He is like a fragile butterfly, perching gently on top of the rocks he wishes to study. He has a young child, I understand, barely a couple of years old before we left for Maoira-I. I suspect this is the reason for his homesickness.

Everyone else has at least one other mission under their belt. The Captain and I have eight between us. I have offered Kimura to sit with us at mealtimes, to perhaps undergo a routine psych evaluation in the infirmary. He refuses all and simply wants to spend time by himself. I do not like that—not on a mission where the five of us need to rely on each other like limbs on the same body—but I will not press him for now. Captain Osoba and I have agreed to keep our doors open for all to approach us whenever, for whatever need.

Everyone else seems to get on with the work. We never leave the Base by ourselves, especially with the presence of wild beasts. Often we will use the Transporter, though we keep this to a minimum as the weather is good and the terrain walkable.

I have walked with everyone and have found Prof. Khan to be the most companionable. He seems at peace with what happens around him, a very grounded man, though not without interesting views on life. I suppose it makes sense, as he is a grandfather, and is in the next stage of life compared to the rest of us. He is a Muslim and adheres very seriously to his faith. On more than one occasion I have accidentally interrupted his daily prayer, but he simply waves it off. He offered me to sit with him on his prayer rug, a woven material that is extremely soft. Other items amongst his personal effects include a tea set, which he uses at least twice a day during his personal time. I have sat with him and drank tea (not my favourite drink of choice, but we were not permitted to bring *that* on spaceflight). It was pleasant, but I suggested we sit outside when the suns were setting. We did so, and now we have our own daily ritual. Aida often joins us, saying it reminds her of home. There is no sunset on Polaris or Vesteris or any of the ships. Perhaps she means the companionable silence that shifts across us between sips of tea.

END OF LOG

MISSION LOG Maoira-I
MISSION 4A
AUTHOR A.B.
Log 32:

We prepared for our second meeting with the Mission. The mission leader for the Maoira-I project is Lieutenant Julian Bishop. I do not care much for him, but the Captain has worked with him on several missions and vouches for his thorough method. The connection during the meeting, however, was patchy and inconsistent. More than once did the vidlink cut out completely. Both Prof. Khan and the Captain are our comms specialists, but even then it was difficult to ascertain what the problem was. They think it is due to the position of the planet; if we face away from the direction of the fleet, as we were this evening, the connection is weaker. We will try again during the day.

END OF LOG

MISSION LOG Maoira-I
MISSION 4A
AUTHOR A.B.
Log 40:

Day 35. I am concerned about Aida. She has vomited twice this morning. We all eat the same rations and have the same water source, so this is not food related. She denies any chance of pregnancy—she and her husband had been trying for several years with no luck, and she had appropriate contraception in the 12 months before spaceflight as she had done for previous planetary missions. But the signs are telling me otherwise.

There is a portable ultrasound unit in the infirmary. She refuses to use this, and this is uncharacteristic of her. I feel she knows what the truth is. I have told her sometimes contraception does not work. I have told her it is not her fault, that this can happen. But we cannot know for sure unless we do an ultrasound.

I have kept this between the two of us for now until the results are confirmed. I do not want to alarm anyone else. If it is true, however, I suspect Aida will want to continue with the pregnancy, as she has waited so long. If that is the case, we must inform the Mission immediately, and an extraction must be planned for both Aida and her baby.

END OF LOG

MISSION LOG Maoira-I
MISSION 4A
AUTHOR A.B.
Log 41:

Day 35, evening. It is confirmed. Aida is around 7-9 weeks pregnant. She is in her dorm and asks for privacy. Aida asked me to tell the crew. She did not want to be present for their reaction.

END OF LOG

MISSION LOG Maoira-I
MISSION 4A
AUTHOR A.B.
Log 45:

Comms have yet to be restored. Prof. Khan and the Captain are working on it, which is beyond my own understanding. The VAS-H is not much use in this aspect; all it can do for now is troubleshoot. Prof. Khan has been working on updating the AI's out-of-date software. I suppose technology moves fast in six years.

This also means that the Mission is not aware of Aida's status. The crew have been supportive, though perhaps shocked at first. She has asked them to treat her the same as they always have. I took her aside after this; she is not the same as she was before. We need to be extra careful with her: a pregnant woman giving birth planetside is unheard of in the fleet's hundreds of years of existence. I am the only medical personnel on this crew and, while

I did not tell her, I am wholly unprepared for this. As a trainee, obstetrics was not my best rotation. I had only just passed by delivering the required number of babies, many with assistance. Two did not survive, and they still haunt me, though I have been told many times it was not my fault. 'These things happen'. I am beginning to see why Aida dislikes that phrase.

END OF LOG

MISSION LOG Maoira-I
MISSION 4A
Log 50:

Day 170. It has been six months since we landed on Maoira-I. I have not kept a log for many months. Comms have not been restored. It is even difficult to send a message via radio.

I have kept Aida on a strict diet and exercise regimen. She is otherwise doing well and was excited when we confirmed the baby is a girl. Aida is still young and as such carries an optimism that, though it is not naive, makes me concerned for her. She wishes beyond anything to share this joy with her husband, but she is equally happy that she has a crew to celebrate with. I am impressed with her optimism, something I would not have shared in her situation. A mother's psychological state during pregnancy can translate into her child. I hope this baby is born as sunny and hopeful as her mother is.

END OF LOG

MISSION LOG Maoira-I
MISSION 4A
AUTHOR A.B.
Log 52:

Communication has been established, though briefly. We have informed Lieutenant Bishop of Aida's condition. We have pushed for an extraction for both mother and baby. He will inform his superiors and speak to us in due course.

END OF LOG

MISSION LOG Maoira-I
MISSION 4A
AUTHOR A.B.
Log 79:

I am not sure what day it is, but a healthy baby girl has been born. She is a little on the slight side, but so is her mother so that is not unexpected. Aida is recovering in her dorm, feeding the infant. Over the past few months she has discussed baby names with us but was yet to settle on one. We are allowing her to rest.

The four of us sat in the kitchen during dinner, an infective sense of elation spreading amongst the crew. Even Shoji was grinning as he filled everyone's glasses with berry juice. He seems far lighter than he has been for the past few months. I hope it continues, for his sake.

END OF LOG

Part Three

Chapter Seventeen

Elif stared at the ceiling for a long time before she realised she was not dreaming. Consciousness came back to her in waves, the slow ebb and flow of her senses until she felt the aches in her body and strain on her mind. Her fever had broken but she was still hot, wrapped under several layers of blankets. She fidgeted until she could free her arms and pulled each layer off. Cool air whipped at her, lashing at her skin even beneath her clothes. Her muscles shook and shivered so she tossed a blanket across her shoulders once more and swung her legs off the bed. A monitor beeped in the dark room, its lights flashing intermittently. Elif rubbed her eyes, stretching out her hand to touch the machine. A vital sign monitor, straight from the infirmary. It was there. How did it get here in the first place? Did VAS-H repair the shell? Impossible. Had she walked in her sleep? That was slightly less impossible. Her limbs twinged and throbbed, body still weak and raw from the illness. It hurt to move an inch. There was no way she would have unconsciously lifted herself off the bed.

Elif tried to speak. She cleared her throat but it hurt like the rest of her body. On a small table next to her bunk was a glass of water. The water looked normal, clear and fresh. Confusion pounded her mind. Did she put the water there herself? There was no way else it would have appeared there. Her throat burned dry so she drank the water almost in one gulp as some spilled down her chin. Even if it was contaminated water, she didn't care.

"Vash," she called out. "How did this monitor get here? And the water?"

"It was brought to your room." VAS-H's voice held the same calmness, but it was skirting the truth.

"How did you bring it to the dorm?" Elif tried to get up from the bed but her muscles protested.

"Oh good, you're awake!" A woman entered the dorm. The lights switched on.

Elif jumped back onto the bunk and shakily stood up, holding the empty glass between her and the woman. This was beyond a hallucination. There was another person in the Base, as if she had walked through the screen from one of her films. The person held a tray with a plate of food. The smell wafted towards Elif, aromatic but different. Her stomach burbled with curiosity. Her mind couldn't keep up with what was happening—was the illness making her hallucinate?

The stranger put the tray down on the side table and raised her hands to show her palms. Her dark hair was cropped just below her ears, her eyes wide and almost black like Elif's. She wore a grey biosuit with a green trim, stained with blood.

There was another person in her home. A wave of nausea shunted through Elif.

"I know this is a shock to you," said the woman, speaking slowly. Her hands remained up high. "My name is Rokeya. I'm an engineer from Polaris. I crash landed here some days ago and found the Base with help of your AI."

The nausea overlapped with a tightness in Elif's chest. She tried to suck in breath, forcing the air into her lungs. Her throat constricted, chest heaved. The edges of her vision blurred before darkening, slowly encroaching on all that she was seeing. The weakness in her legs crept up, spilling into all her muscles until it reached her head. Elif dropped down into the bed and all went dark.

*

When she woke for the second time, the woman sat in a chair across the room. Elif gripped the blanket and shuffled back into the wall, wanting to put as much distance between her and the stranger. But the woman did not move. Her head lolled on her shoulder, eyes fluttering in sleep. The tray of food remained on the table, but the smell wasn't as strong now. Elif edged towards the plate, keeping an eye on the stranger, and looked at the food. The cabbage she had grown was cut into fine strips and cooked into a dull brown broth with chunks of potato. Elif sniffed it. She wanted to throw up. Forcing herself up, she slipped out of the bed and ran out the dorm, almost crying out in pain.

"Vash! Emergency!" She ran into the control room and locked the door. "What... is happening?" Words scattered from her mouth as Elif tried to catch her breath.

"Young Elif, I have verified the engineer's credentials. She is who she says she is."

A throb pulsated in Elif's head. "None of this makes sense. I don't want someone else here and I thought that was how we left it. And why did we receive no other information? Why is she here!"

"The engineer known as 'Rokeya' has been most useful. She has fixed the water filtration unit, tended to you as you were unconscious—"

"She did what?" Elif dropped down into the chair. A stronger wave of muscle aches came back, burning fire across her arms and legs.

"You were severely dehydrated. She drip fed you water every thirty minutes, without delay or interruption. She gave you pain and fever relief for the last three days." Elif said nothing, so VAS-H continued. "She is also wounded herself and has not slept well since her arrival."

A gentle knock echoed at the door. There was no viewing port, no way to look outside. Another knock.

"Why is she here?" she hissed. "What does she want?"

"She appears to have made an emergency landing. Her ship crashed in the forest."

But why would she even want to come here? It was too difficult to think, to come up with any answer. Elif wheeled the chair over to the door and cleared her sore throat.

"Who are you?" she called out, wincing at how small her voice sounded. "What do you want?"

"Well, right now, I want you to eat. You're nothing but skin and bones, Elif."

The air snatched from her lungs. "How do you know my name?"

It was a stupid question, but she couldn't stop turning her name over in the stranger's voice. Not like it was in VAS-H's monotone drawl.

"Why are you here?"

"I crash landed, but I wanted to come here. I was assigned this mission some time ago."

Elif wanted to open the door and stare at this impossible human, to gaze at every crevice and artefact across the woman's face, every wrinkle and spot. She had the strangest urge to reach out through the door and touch her, to make sure she was real. Elif raised her hand to wave her bio-print over the scan-lock before deciding against it.

"That was years ago, and it was cancelled. You expect me to just welcome you with open arms? You expect me to just be alright with this?"

There was silence on the other side of the door, then some shuffling that echoed further and further away. Some moments later, something heavy dropped on the floor by the door before the shuffling echoed once more down the hall.

Chapter Eighteen

The Base held a quiet that Elif could not trust. Home did not feel the same, its air disturbed with an unwelcome presence. She sat uncomfortably on the chair, legs draped over the armrest as she drifted in and out of sleep. There were no more knocks at the door. Even VAS-H did not interrupt her slumber.

Eventually, nature called. She opened the door quietly and glanced around the hall before stepping out. Her foot landed on the tray, missing the bowl of broth by a few inches. Elif winced at the clatter echoing down the hall. Nothing else stirred in its wake.

"Vash," she called out in the lavatory cubicle. "Should I engage with her?"

A beat of silence. "She does not mean any harm."

"How do you know that?"

"Aside from possibly saving your life?"

I don't like that answer, she thought as she washed her hands. She didn't want to be indebted to someone else. The flowing water was cool and fresh. The filtration unit was fixed then, as it had been blocked the day the illness retired her to bed.

The stranger was fast asleep in the infirmary, body sagging into the contours of the sick bed. Elif crept inside, careful not to make any noise. She had never used the infirmary beds for her own use, always finding them too cold and uncomfortable.

The woman was less threatening when asleep, though no less strange. Her skin was a few shades darker than Elif's, short hair tucked behind her ears. One of her ears had a silver ring on its outer edge. There were dots across her chin, scars of some kind of illness. She slept curled up, as if trying to conserve space, legs folded and arms tucked in. The bandage on her right arm was stained red. Her face looked exhausted, dark circles beneath closed eyes, drained of all energy. Elif thought of the broth outside the control room, how wisps of its aroma drifted towards her when it was first offered. She was so used to eating the vegetables raw, out of necessity more than taste. Elif wanted to ask about this and so much more, but she dared not.

When Rokeya's eyes opened, Elif's limbs became rigid. She leant against the opposite bed.

"Are you going to run away again?" the woman asked quietly. She remained curled up.

Elif shook her head slowly, gripping the edge of the bed behind her.

"Did you eat?"

Elif shook her head again. She looked away from the stranger, finding the eye contact too strong, but forced herself to stay put.

"Where did you come from?" she asked.

"Polaris. It's the capital city-ship of the fleet." Rokeya smiled. "Is it my turn for a question?"

Elif nodded but kept her distance.

"Are you feeling better?"

Elif paused. "Better than a few days ago. Still tired. Still weak."

Rokeya nodded understandingly.

"How did you hurt your arm?" asked Elif.

"Some broken glass from my ship. It's healing for now, but I am worried about an infection. You got any antibiotics around here?"

Elif shook her head. "All used up. We never received much from the Mission."

Rokeya scoffed. "Ah right, I see they've extended the antibiotic shortage even down to you..."

"What do you mean?"

Rokeya swung herself upright and rubbed her eyes. "It's difficult to keep manufacturing antibiotics to keep up with the strains of bacteria on the fleet. We have to limit our use of them otherwise none of them will ever work. Any infection must be confirmed as bacterial before antibiotics are given."

All this information washed through Elif like a wave that wouldn't stop. She could feel her lungs struggle to take in air. She closed her eyes and bowed her head.

"Are you okay?" asked Rokeya.

Elif nodded. "I'm going back to sleep. Please don't come into my dorm. I need space."

*

The next three days passed in a haze. Elif spent most of the time in her dorm, drifting in and out of sleep. She would find the tray outside the door on her way to the lavatory, laden with cooked vegetables and boiled potatoes. By the end of the third day, most of her strength was back and her mind had finally cleared. She no longer wanted to spend all day in bed.

Elif found Rokeya in the control room. She stayed outside the threshold but cleared her throat, unsure how to interrupt. Rokeya swivelled round on the chair and smiled warmly. It was unnerving.

"You look well! All that sleep must be doing you good."

"What are you doing here?" asked Elif. "This is the control room; you shouldn't be in here."

Rokeya nodded but turned back around to the set of monitors. "I know you don't like me in your space, but I wanted to check everything was running smoothly."

Elif scowled, the insult digging deep inside her. "I don't need your help! I've run this place since—"

"I know, I know. But you're not feeling well, so I'm just helping out—"

"You need to leave now." She'd force this intruder out if she had to. "You're not welcome here."

Rokeya let out a laugh before she saw the young woman's expression. Her smile dissolved into a frown.

"Elif, you've been doing this on your own for too long. That's not right; you shouldn't have had to. You shouldn't even *be* on this planet by yourself. But now I'm here."

"No, you're not here. You crash landed here and made yourself at home. You need to leave."

Rokeya rose from the chair, her right hand gripped into a fist. Elif took a step back.

"I'm sorry you feel that way, but it's not as easy as that. I can't just 'leave'. I have to wait for a mission crew to respond to my distress signal, and that can take anywhere between a day or a month."

"*You sent a distress signal?*" Elif's chest tightened. "No no no... no no no..."

"What's the problem?" said Rokeya. "That's the only way I can return to Polaris, and obviously we can't just leave you here..."

"I'm not leaving, I can't leave, this isn't right—"

"Where did you find this?" Rokeya uncurled her fist. Inside her palm sat the silver ring she had discovered years ago. Elif had forgotten about its mystery since it didn't do anything.

"That's not yours, I found it." She made to swipe it before Rokeya snatched her hand away. For the first time Elif realised how much taller the engineer was to her, with broader shoulders and a surety settled in her posture that she couldn't match. For the first time in years, she felt small again. Insignificant. Not worthy of her space. Elif bit back her tears and ran towards the airlock.

Polaris

—Jaflong District, Aremu compound

Isobel Aremu sat on her legs, the earth beneath her soft. Her hands shook as she tried to grip the trowel, but her swollen joints would not allow her to. She placed the tool beside her and stared at them. Over the years her fingers had morphed to take a strange, gnarled shape. Her thumbs were the worst. Inflammatory arthritis, the doctors had said. Medication slowed it down, but on her worst days the pain was unbearable. Isobel had never felt sorry for herself, would never allow herself pity. But the former Commander wondered if the arthritic joints was her form of atonement for the decision she'd made all those years ago. Isobel was not a religious woman, would only look God's way in those rare moments of desperation. In retirement, she kept those moments to a barer minimum than before. There was nothing worse than wallowing in despair in the calm of your elder years.

The doorbell rang. It took some effort to get up from where she sat, and a few more grunts to stumble her way through the house with a stiff back.

"Julian," she said once she'd opened the door. "I thought we'd agreed not to meet at my home."

"Needed to get away from it all," he said, almost forcing his way in.

The mighty Julian Bishop had crawled with his tail between his legs a few times into her home office in the past year. Retirement had treated her with mercy, yet the years had not been kind to Commander Bishop. She watched as the lines across his pale face were more pronounced, his skin unusually shiny. His lips had disappeared, his mouth a spurious straight line. Isobel was sure he'd got some kind of cosmetic treatment. She sat on a chair opposite him, ignoring her desk, and glanced at the floor-length mirror fixed to the wall. Perhaps time was not her enemy; she may have been a grandmother but her dark skin was plump, wrinkles only at the edges of her eyes. But Isobel did not want to cast a moral aspersion. They were both at fault, and they knew it. And yet she allowed Julian Bishop into her home every so often, to purge their sins in secrecy.

"We've received a distress signal," he said.

"From?" A useless question. "It's the stolen ship, isn't it? Did we ever identify the—"

"Rokeya Haddad. Latif Khan's granddaughter."

Isobel accepted the silence as it came, heavy and punishing. Were the ghosts of the crew haunting them now, from graves in another world?

"And the signal?"

"Strong and clear. It seems the connection is the strongest during the spring season, with fewer atmospheric interferences." He shifted in his seat, directing his entire attention to Isobel. "The signal is enough to be picked up from external receivers."

She nodded. More groups had sprouted in the past six years, demanding the return of the child born on Maoira-I. No information was officially disclosed by the Mission, but there were enough leaks, especially in the beginning. And when an innocuous stasis ship was missing from the hangar bay's inventory, it was enough to cause a panic. Who would be stupid enough to fly, unaccompanied, for half-a-decade to a world where it was likely all were dead? Whoever the mystery pilot was, they were hailed as a hero. Groups of people with unlicensed radio receivers had stationed themselves in pockets around Polaris—and Isobel had heard the other cities too—awaiting the signal from the hero pilot. And here it was. The Mission could no longer stay silent, nor could they ignore it.

"And once she returns..." Her words evaporated in the thick silence.

"Which one?" A dry smirk cracked Julian's face.

"We'll have to tell her," said Isobel, "About the crew. About their deaths, what happened. Your ridiculous idea of creating a fake position, a 'Warden', to give her purpose."

"You approved of the idea at the time—"

"The child needed nurturing, Julian, not a job. Sometimes I think we gave her a title only to relieve ourselves from giving her a proper childhood."

He glared at her, the pupils constricting.

"And we will need to inform the public too. It was not our fault; it was a perfect storm of improbable conditions."

Julian leaned forward and placed a hand on the side of her chair.

"They won't see it that way. None of them will. You know what people are like. Always eager for an execution."

Isobel was not sure whether it was the execution that people thirsted for or the idea that someone had been held culpable. He leaned back in his chair, the tension between his eyes relaxing a fraction. Isobel shifted in her seat; the air had changed, now charged with an idea.

"And how do we prepare for an execution?" she asked.

"We give them someone to hang."

"Surely you are not suggesting me? You made the final call at the end of the day—"

"We can go over the events another time; we've done it before. You were Commander at the time, nothing can change that." He leaned forwards again. "And you're getting older. Weary. Tired. You can barely walk without moaning about your back. You have grandchildren."

Isobel scoffed. "Are you suggesting a PR campaign around how I look, Julian?"

"They will go far more easily on you than they ever would on me. I know how people view me, the impression I make on others. Your sentence would be far lighter than mine."

"I'm not taking the fall—"

"You won't have to."

She was beginning to get irritated with how often he interrupted her. Or was she simply allowing him to? Had age really taken its toll, making her more docile, content with the bare minimum?

"You won't be taking the fall. You'll be coming forward, volunteering information. You'll be atoning for your mistakes. The Mission will stay the villain, as it always has been. But this way we give the public something to chew on."

"I will not be your bait, Julian." Isobel stood up sharply, ignoring the aches in her joints. "You should leave. And next time, don't bother ringing the bell. I won't be answering."

Chapter Nineteen

The girl still had not returned to the Base after nightfall, which VAS-H confirmed was out of the ordinary. They travelled side by side again and returned to the forest once more, VAS-H controlling the Transporter as Rokeya walked beside it. After a while, Rokeya grew tired, her body still weak from injury. She asked for permission to climb aboard the vehicle, finding it strange to ask an AI for approval. She wasn't sure she liked it.

The Transporter trundled across the forest floor at an agonisingly slow pace. Rokeya kept the door open, calling out Elif's name every so often. There was no answer save for the chirp of insects that filled the trees, the squawk of native birds, the rustle of small creatures. The tyres ran smoothly until the terrain changed and Rokeya felt rattles and shakes as they drove over larger bumps.

"What's happening?" she asked.

"We are approaching the crater," said VAS-H, its voice tinny.

The Transporter came to a stop. Rokeya jumped out, pausing for a long moment at the edge of the forest. The view was spectacular. The dark silhouettes of large trees grew all around the crater's rim which ran for at least four miles. The crater itself was rough and rocky, its length twice as long as its width. An asteroid's last mark on a silent planet, it would take the better part of a day to cross the crater. The Transporter's headlamps did not offer much light across the breadth of such a large landmark.

"Maybe she went around the crater?" said Rokeya. She took a few steps forward, the absolute edge of the cliff a mere inch away from her feet. The way down was steep, the large hole of the basin an incredible void. Rokeya felt a strange urge come over her to jump into the crater.

The Transporter edged slightly closer to her, snapping her out of those thoughts. Its lights shone down the steep walls. There, on a narrow ledge just a few feet below, was Elif. She squinted at the light, holding her hand up to shield her eyes.

"Elif!" Rokeya dropped down to her hands and knees, the rough ground scraping her palms. "We'll lift you out of there."

"It's no use," she called out, voice weary and strained. "I'm too far away. And I've done something to my ankle... it twisted as I fell down. I can't move."

Rokeya turned to the Transporter. "Is there a way to lift me down?"

VAS-H's voice echoed from within. "Negative. All methods would be dangerous. There is no safe way to drop down onto the ledge. And there are no materials on the Transporter that could be used to drop you down."

She couldn't just leave the girl there, all by herself. Rokeya grabbed on to the grille at the front of the Transporter and hoisted herself up to the hood of the vehicle. She instructed VAS-H to drive forward until she hung over the dark void, Elif's thin silhouette somewhere below her. Holding tightly to the grille, Rokeya lowered herself, gingerly feeling for a foothold in the crumbling wall of the crater.

"You're going to hurt yourself!" called out Elif.

It was the first time she had shown any type of concern for Rokeya, but the engineer put that to the back of her mind. Irregular rocks and pebbles stuck out from the wall, some better to hold on to than others. Rokeya gripped the nearest one to her face before deciding it was too smooth; another small rock with a jagged edge was better placed as a handhold. Sweat slid down her back inside her biosuit as she struggled to hold her own bodyweight. Her hands were bleeding. The muscles in her arms were at breaking point.

"How far down are you?" she called out to Elif. Before the girl could answer, her sweaty palms fumbled and Rokeya tumbled down. She landed on the narrow ledge on her side with a thump and a shriek from Elif.

"Oh no oh no oh no," stammered Elif. "Are you okay?"

She had rolled to the side just as Rokeya fell, leaving her precariously on the edge. Rokeya grabbed her arm and yanked the girl towards the wall.

"I'm fine; luckily didn't land on my arm. Vash, can you give us some more light down here?"

Elif's ankle was swollen and red, but the girl wasn't crying out in pain. That was a good sign.

"We just need to avoid putting any pressure on it." Rokeya sat back against the jagged wall, her chest heaving.

"But how are we going to get back up there? Why did you come down here? You should have gone back to Base for something to pull me out!" Elif folded her arms. Her hair had fallen out of its ponytail, now a tangled mess around her gaunt, frowning face.

"I couldn't just leave you here," said Rokeya. "How on earth did you end up down here anyway?"

"I fell," came the sullen response.

"That doesn't sound very sensible of someone like you."

Elif looked up, cheeks slightly reddened. "I'm not lying."

"I didn't say you were," said Rokeya. A lighter blue brushed across the edges of the trees, surrounding them in a delicate halo. Daylight would be upon them in a few hours. "Look, I'm sorry for just barging in on your home. I wasn't actually expecting there to be anyone here. I was looking for... for information."

Elif raised her head from her chest. "Information? What kind of information?"

"I have no idea where you came from, Elif, but there was a crewed mission to Maoira-I many years ago. The Mission lost contact with them. My grandfather was part of that crew.

"I was assigned to this planet about five or six years ago, but that project was pulled from me as quickly as it was assigned. All access to information regarding Maoira-I was restricted."

Elif shuffled slightly on the rough ground. It was difficult to get comfortable on a windy ledge, difficult to put a gap between the two of them. She seemed to want to maintain that gap.

"So you came here to find him?"

"I know he's not alive. He was in his sixties when he accepted the position on the crew. But I just want to find out what happened to him. My parents live on Vesteris, another city, so I don't get to see them that often. He's the only other family I have. *Had.*"

"What are your parents like?" The question came so innocently, so suddenly it nearly knocked Rokeya off the ledge. She had expected to keep defending her presence.

She fumbled for the words. "Uh, well, they're nice?"

Elif looked at her blankly. Rokeya cleared her throat. "My dad's pretty typical, makes 'dad jokes' all the time, tries to make sure everyone's happy. Kind of like me, I guess. My mother is like her father, my grandfather, quiet and always concentrating on something."

"I don't know anything about my family." Elif tucked her hair behind her ears. "I was never told anything. I have no clue where I came from. I mean, Vash's always been here, but does an AI count as family?"

Rokeya wanted to answer, wanted to let Elif know just how wrong it was that she was left on Maoira-I to fend for herself. She thought better of it.

"We'll need to figure out how to get out of this dirt bowl once it gets light enough. Get some rest for now."

Chapter Twenty

Elif awoke with the suns rising in her eyes. Golden light washed across the rock formations, their stark shadows bleeding into the crater's floor. Her mouth was stale and dry. Her ankle throbbed, though not as much as it had before. The swelling had gone down but her skin was still red, and she didn't like the look of it. Elif looked directly above the ledge to see the Transporter's headlamps positioned down at them but switched off. She wondered what VAS-H did in the time they'd fallen asleep.

Rokeya sat slumped next to her, chin resting on her chest. She looked like a doll someone had thrown, legs splayed and arms limp. Her chest rose and fell gently, deep in sleep. Daylight flickered across her hair, revealing glints of maroon in the black. Elif looked at her own locks, long and unkempt, and wondered if Rokeya had been born with hair like that.

Elif peered over the edge of the ledge. It was a steep drop down, and she didn't want to risk another injury.

"You're not thinking of jumping down there yourself?"

Elif jumped at Rokeya's rough voice. The woman rubbed her eyes, yawning loudly into the cool morning air. The sound carried across the crater, bouncing across its walls.

Rokeya shivered and rubbed her hands on the opposite arms. "Aren't you cold?"

Elif shrugged. "Wouldn't it be easier to climb back up?"

"On what?" said Rokeya. They both craned their necks up at the same time. "Those rocks aren't very useful if gravity is working against us."

"So what... we're climbing *down* on them?"

"I'm afraid so, kiddo. But it's alright, I'll go first. You can fall on me if you like."

*

Elif's arm was curled around Rokeya's neck. She tried not to put all her weight on Rokeya, didn't particularly want to touch her either, but she managed to limp with her support. The engineer was a few inches taller than her, putting them at an awkward angle. But Elif couldn't walk alone as she could barely put pressure on her foot without the pain biting into her bones. So they limp-walked their way across the crater as sunlight beat down on their faces.

When Rokeya first took Elif's hand, the young woman expected a shock, a tremble, something significant. Her breath caught in her throat. She'd never touched another person before. But the moment was so ordinary, so mundane, that she was almost disappointed. Now, as she felt Rokeya's grip tighten on her fingers, she marvelled at the types of pressure the human touch could exhibit. It was nothing like holding on to VAS-H's now-defunct metal shell, and it was completely different to the soft, velvety leaves that grew in the Garden. Rokeya's skin was dry and hard, but her hands were warm.

The crater looked much like how the land appeared during the dead season. Rainwater hadn't touched the ground; either that or something was preventing the forest from taking over across the crater. They walked close to the eastern wall, observing the perimeter for any shallower exit points, but this meant taking the long way round.

"Let's stop here," said Rokeya, setting Elif down on a bumpy rock. "Just for a few minutes."

Tall outcroppings of rock stood above them like statues, their shadows large and looming. The wind whipped across the walls, zigzagging between the outcroppings. It felt cooler down here than the forest. Elif took a big deep breath; she'd never tire of breathing fresh air.

"What's a dad joke?" she asked, breaking the soft silence.

Rokeya blinked at her, puzzled, before chuckling. "It's a joke, but like a really obvious one. It's so obvious that it's not even funny."

Elif nodded, not really understanding. "So why would someone say a joke that's not funny?"

Rokeya grinned. "That's why they call them dad jokes! Because only your dad would be silly enough to say them out loud." As soon as she'd said it, Rokeya's grin fell away, dissolving into regret. "Oh no, I mean, I completely get why you wouldn't get it..."

Elif shrugged. "It's okay. I don't really know what life would be like with parents."

As she spoke, something ached inside her. It was that strange longing again, that gnawing emptiness that had grown inside her for the past few years. It grew bigger with Rokeya's presence, as the woman's laughter echoed through the crater. Elif felt like she missed something that didn't exist.

Rokeya came to sit next to her.

"You know that's not right? I don't even know what the hell the Mission were thinking, putting a baby on a planet all on its own. What kind of sick person does that?"

Rokeya stared at the ground in front of them, her voice getting steadily louder. Elif shrunk into the rock, shoulders wilting, as if something was her fault.

"... such idiots running the show, they have no idea what it's like being on the ground—"

Rokeya caught herself and glanced over at a silent Elif.

"Sorry... I have a lot of feelings about the Mission. *Clearly.* Let's just keep moving."

She offered her hand to Elif. The younger woman looked at it warily; the creases on Rokeya's palm were covered in dirt and dried blood. The urge to run away trembled within all her muscles, but her leg was out of commission. She had no other choice. She slipped her hand into Rokeya's warm one and grimaced as the engineer hoisted her arm over her neck.

*

The midday heat had filtered down into the cracks and crevices of the crater. Both of them decided it was a good idea to take a break and wait the heat out. They first sought shelter in the narrow shadows of the tall rocks before Rokeya spotted a small opening in the northeastern wall. It was a cave, and it was likely to be cooler than the rest of the crater.

Everything about the cave was uneven and jagged; the entrance was not so much a rounded hole but a gash in the rocky wall, like a scar. Inside, sunlight barely filtered in. Rokeya raised her left hand. A bright light flashed from her wrist, illuminating the walls in a harsh white glow.

"Let's rest here," said Rokeya.

Her voice carried through the small cave. Elif could hear the rush of water somewhere far away, perhaps deeper inside.

She limped to the other side, glad to be free of the other woman, until her foot caught on a bump in the ground. She shrieked as she fell, hands outstretched as she tumbled to the floor. Rokeya shouted her name.

"I'm fine," said Elif, catching her breath. "What is that?"

The wristlight shone on the ground. Shadows danced across the walls. The ground was uneven, dipping and rising, until Elif realised these were not natural dips. The mounds were manmade, each one a few feet long. At the top of each mound was a small stone, a rock no bigger than her hand. Something felt familiar about these, as if she had read or watched a docu-series about—

"They're graves," said Rokeya. "It's the crew."

Chapter Twenty-One

Rokeya was eight years old when she saw her first, and only, dead body. Her grandmother had passed away quietly in the night and the family whisked themselves away on a special permit visit to Vesteris for the funeral. Rokeya remembered seeing her dadu's wrinkled face set in powder and smelling of some kind of disinfectant. Dadu had been paler than usual, the powder blanching her usual almond skin. The ends of her lips were always turned downwards in a perpetual frown. As a girl, Rokeya had the strangest urge to reach into the casket and push that frown away, to make sure her grandmother wasn't spending all eternity in sadness.

They were meant to say goodbye when they visited the casket. Rokeya's father had bent down over the box, placing a gentle kiss on his mother's forehead. She was ushered forward to face the dead body herself and say her final goodbye. Rokeya had felt awkward but copied her father's motion of kissing her forehead. Only Rokeya's lips never touched her grandmother's skin; no, she was too scared she would wake her up and she'd receive a scolding. Instead she whispered '*bye Dadu*' and skipped back to her own mother to stand in place for the funeral.

Funeral rites on the fleet encompassed the different customs of humanity, but the ships could only offer so much space within the morgues. Originally it was a spaceflight custom to preserve the bodies until they found a planet of habitation. Once this seemed like a more distant dream, officials mandated to choose your method of burial upon reaching eighteen years of age: be shot out to space, cremated for fuel or undergo rapid decomposition for fertile soil to grow food. Only the truly wealthy could afford a space in the vaults of the morgues.

Rokeya dropped to her knees and placed a hand on the edge of the nearest grave. "There's only four graves."

"So?" said Elif, the unease obvious on her face.

"So there were five people on the crew. There's a missing grave."

"Or maybe that person didn't die."

Rokeya glanced at her darkly. Perhaps it was possible. The youngest crew member, Shoji Kimura, was only twenty-eight before spaceflight. But where else would he, or any of them, have gone? And why were these graves so far away from the Base, where no one, not even sunlight or rainwater, could reach them? A strange urge came over her, to unearth the person beneath each grave with her hands and beckon them to wake. To see the face of her grandfather again, powdered now with dirt and dust, and plant a kiss on his forehead.

"What are you doing?" Elif's sharp voice cut through her thoughts.

Rokeya watched as her outstretched hand had turned into a claw, fingers digging into the dried dirt. She snatched it back.

"Sorry. I just... I didn't think I'd find graves. I thought... well, I don't know what I thought."

"So these people were here before me?" asked Elif in the dark. "I don't understand, I'm the Warden of Maiora-I. Why would these people be here long enough to die?"

Rokeya spoke into the darkness. "Vash mentioned this too. What's a Warden? And why are you so... obsessed with the title?"

A shuffle. Perhaps a scowl. "That's what I am. It's an important role. I have to look after everything, I have to... *a warden is someone who is in charge of or cares for or has custody over persons, animals or things. Or, the highest executive officer in charge of a prison.*" There it was, that dictionary definition again. "That's what every planet of interest has. That's what Commander Aremu told me when I first spoke to her."

It dawned on Rokeya that this was another lie that the Mission had cast over the planet. Not for the citizens of the fleet, but the lone citizen of Maiora-I.

"When did you first speak to her?"

"When I was twelve."

"And before that?"

A pause. "What do you mean?"

"Who did you speak to before Commander Aremu? Before you were twelve years old?"

"No one. Just Vash. And I watched a lot of movies. And read a lot. I didn't need anyone else."

Anger burned inside Rokeya's chest, spreading through to her limbs. She wanted to smash the wall of the cave, but that wouldn't have helped anything. It might have scared Elif. She turned the wristlight on again and aimed it towards the ceiling. Elif's face was mostly shadows in its thin beam of light, but it was better than nothing. She shuffled towards the girl, feeling the heaviness of breaking bad news.

"Elif, you should never have been here on your own. I think... I think one of the crew was your mother. Maybe one of them was your father, I don't know. There are strict protocols in place for these things, precisely for this reason. But you were born on this world through no fault of your own, and suddenly everyone else disappeared. You were left here all by yourself." She wanted to reach out, pull the girl in for a tight hug, never let her go again. "You need to come back home. Where there are people, where you have a family."

Elif did not move. She stared as Rokeya spoke, a sudden confidence in her dark eyes.

"I am home."

The words hung in the air like weighted spears turned towards Rokeya. She feared moving would hurl them straight at her. Instead Elif staggered to stand, using the walls for support. She limped away from Rokeya, small shoulders squared, and slipped back through the narrow entrance.

Chapter Twenty-Two

They walked in silence for another hour. Elif refused to take a break, not wanting to be inside the crater for a moment longer than she had to. She reluctantly held on to Rokeya's shoulder with each painful limp. She was sick of Rokeya, sick of her presence that hurtled into her world like an asteroid—reckless, explosive, selfish. And then there was the distress signal that she'd triggered: what if they forced her to leave Maoira-I, to 'return' to Polaris? She could barely adjust to another person, forget a whole society.

At the fall of dusk, they'd found an exit. A shallow dip in the crater's walls but still a climb, though less steep than the drop they'd first found themselves in. Instead of clinging on to smooth rocks they simply had to haul themselves up on to several ledges, like a staircase built for a giant. Once at the top, Elif fell flat on the ground, groaning over her injured foot. Climbing hadn't done her ankle any favours. Rokeya crouched over her, face shrouded in the darkening light of the sky. Elif was sure the older woman had been crying.

"Are you alright? Do you want me to go get Vash? Maybe we could get a ride back to the Base."

Elif shook her head fiercely. "There's no point. It'll be double the wait."

"But you can barely walk, and I don't think I can carry you that far right now." Rokeya looked around the dark forest, as if expecting there to be a solution in the shadows. She shone her wristlight into the thicket. Its harsh glow had dimmed since its first use. It was losing light.

"I'll be back, stay here," said Rokeya before she slinked off into the forest.

Where else am I going, thought Elif.

Some moments later Rokeya returned with the slim trunk of a sapling held in both hands, fresh roots covered in thick blobs of dirt. The upper part of the trunk had a few branches. Rokeya snapped off the thinner ones and threw them to the ground.

"You can use this," she said, offering the tree trunk to Elif. "As a walking aid. You can use me as well but at least this way we can both get back in one piece."

The trunk worked surprisingly well, though it was a little too long. The branch end dug into Elif's armpit and chafed at the skin beneath her shirt. But limping wasn't as painful as it had been before. The two walked side by side once again under the stars, skirting the slim edge between trees and crater. The buzz of the forest insects grew louder, palpating the silence between the two women.

"I'm sorry about what I said before," said Rokeya. "This is your home. You were born here, so it makes sense."

Elif grunted as she adjusted the trunk beneath her arm. "It's fine."

"No, it's not. None of this is fine."

"Why are you so obsessed with why I'm here?" Elif tried her best to restrain the bite in her words. "It's got nothing to do with you."

"Because people should be held accountable for the things they do wrong. They should apologise. Wrongs should be righted, as best we can. And if they can't be righted, we should make sure they don't happen again."

The air around them grew thicker, almost suffocating Elif. She wasn't sure how to respond. She just wanted to go back to silence, to focus on her hunger, exhaustion and the pain in her ankle. It was strange that this woman, with no connection to her, was trying to help her, through no motivation but kindness. It was another constraint, to be indebted to someone else. But was that what Rokeya was asking for? She was not expecting an exchange of resources. She simply wanted to help.

Elif grunted as she limped. Those four graves back in the cave—she refused to believe she had come from one of them. That one, or two, could have been her parent, could have protected her and loved her and given her everything that the Mission never did. Tears pricked at the edges of her eyes. A lump formed in her throat. It was too much to think about. She wanted to get back to Base, back to her dorm, back to VAS-H's monotone voice. She wanted Rokeya gone but she wanted to curl up inside her warm hands too. She wanted too much—Elif was exhausted.

For the last third of the walk, Rokeya insisted Elif lean on her instead as the rough trunk was cutting into her skin. Once they saw the Transporter with its dim headlamps, Elif could have cried in relief. She nearly pushed away from Rokeya, wanting to run into the vehicle and not come out, but she restrained herself to limp beside her helper.

"Aren't you a sight for sore eyes," said Rokeya, helping Elif get into the seat inside. "Hope it wasn't too boring out here."

"No," said VAS-H, "But the Transporter's battery was running low so I returned to Base to recharge before coming back."

Elif pressed her head against the headrest and closed her eyes. For a small moment, she didn't care what the other two were talking about. She just wanted to be carried back to bed and for once, she could afford to think that.

"That's some initiative," said Rokeya. "You're a strange kind of AI, Vash."

The buzzing of insects filled the air.

"Your distress signal has received a response. A rescue effort has been accepted."

Chapter Twenty-Three

"A distress signal? No no, no one can come here, no that's bad, that's so bad..."

Elif held her head in her hands as she spoke, her breathing heavy. Rokeya watched as the girl descended into panic. She held out a hand.

"Elif, look at me."

The girl's eyes snapped up, wide with fear, her eyebrows wilted.

"Can I take your hand?"

Elif did not speak, perhaps could not speak, but nodded shakily. Rokeya climbed into the vehicle and sat on her knees beside the seat. Elif's hands were still glued to her head, so Rokeya gently peeled one off and intertwined their fingers. Rokeya squeezed, gently but firmly, and watched as Elif crumpled into a lump on the seat. Her chest heaved, heavy breaths but now slower. They stayed that way for a few moments, hands still together. And then she felt a squeeze back. It was light, not as firm as her own, but it was there.

Half an hour later, Elif sat forward and let go of Rokeya's hand. She bit the inside of her cheek, worry in her dark eyes.

"You won't go anywhere if you don't want to," said Rokeya calmly. "But I need to go home, even if you stay."

Elif nodded.

"Vash?" said Rokeya. "We're good now. Let's get going again."

No answer. Rokeya called the AI's name twice more before asking Elif to tap the black screen. A menu came up, unlike before. Despite the lights that filled the vehicle and the hum of the engine, there was a strange emptiness inside.

"What's wrong?" said Elif.

"Does Vash sometimes... disappear from here? Go back to the Base?"

"No, the software is too old to hold up against a gap in connection like that. We'd have to be within a certain proximity to the Base for Vash to safely upload back into the building, right Vash?" No answer. "Vash?"

"I don't think—"

Elif toggled with the controls, calling out the AI's name. "Oh no no no no..."

"Elif, I'm sure—"

"Shut up, just shut up. We need to get back home."

Rokeya feared another panic attack. She reached out to hold Elif's hand again but the girl had already put the vehicle in motion. She operated the Transporter with an expertise that belied her stature, driving fast and without care for the trees coming their way or the dip in the hill that appeared suddenly.

"Slow down," said Rokeya, sure that her words would be ignored. "We'll crash into the building!"

Elif said nothing, though her hand eased on the accelerator lever, her good foot gently pressing on the brake. They came to a sharp stop just outside the airlock entrance. Without bothering to wait for it to open, Elif scrambled out of the Transporter, nearly climbing over Rokeya. One hand held on to the door for support as Elif stared at the building.

The entire Base was cloaked in darkness.

*

The airlock would not open. The girl hopped on one leg towards the hatch, striking it with her fists in desperation, calling out VAS-H's name.

Rokeya had an inkling of an idea of what was happening, and why it was happening, but that didn't answer the *why now*? She dropped out of the vehicle and placed a hand on Elif's shoulder. The girl flinched away from her.

"You know there's a manual key, right here?" Rokeya pointed at a small box next to the door.

When they had entered the Base, they were met with a wall of darkness. Only emergency green lights lined the sides of the hallways. Rokeya held Elif's arm over her shoulder as the two of them staggered towards the core processor room. There was no use shouting VAS-H's name here: the AI had long since been silenced.

The core processor room was cramped and dark. The processor itself was a slim and narrow machine with a few flashing white lights. Rokeya had seen plenty of these installed. Elif dropped to her knees to examine a certain piece of circuitry. Her face looked younger in the wash of white-blue glow from the unit's single screen.

"It's still on, so Vash must still be in here," muttered the girl.

"Elif," said Rokeya gently as she joined her on the floor. "You do know about the Restoration Directive, right?"

"Of course," she snapped. "That doesn't apply here."

"Why not?"

Elif glared at Rokeya, and the older woman felt like she was a speck of dirt on a pristine plate.

"Because I reprogrammed the software to remove that," she said, enunciating each word with hate. "Because I made sure that Vash wouldn't expire as long as I'm here."

"You can't override the Directive." It took all of Rokeya's energy to keep her voice neutral. "Even my grandfather tried, in his research. It's a fixed part of the code. If you remove it, you'll break the interface between an adaptable AI and what it's housed in." *You'll kill VAS-H if you're not careful.*

"Maybe your grandfather wasn't as smart as you thought he was."

Rokeya bit her tongue. Not here, not now.

"Maybe," she said, "but the point is, the Directive is in play now. You can't override it."

She paused over the next words, hesitant to speak them into the already fragile air. "Vash is gone."

"Vash can't be gone, an AI can't just die, their memory is always there somewhere, and if the processor is still running then they're still there..." Elif muttered to herself as she opened up a panel and examined some wires.

Rokeya shuffled back on her knees to look at the room, flashing her wristlight across the walls. Several white sheets were drawn over dozens of boxes. She pulled a sheet away and peered inside. The boxes were filled with items: empty plant pots, digital photo frames, a tea set, collections of CDs with film titles that were far older than Rokeya, a chess set, more CDs titled 'LOGS', a few blankets, several boxes filled with clothes, a thick prayer mat. She brushed her fingertips across the woven material.

"This is all their stuff," she whispered. "Why would it be hidden away?"

Rokeya pulled the mat out of the box. A CD fell on the floor with a clatter, the words 'FOR VAS-H' written on its case in an untidy scrawl. A lump formed in Rokeya's throat, her stomach sick with longing. She knew whose writing that was.

Interlude III

Dear VAS-H,

We were supposed to write logs but I never did that. I have not written a single word in the past year and a half except to update your code. I find it strange to write to no one in particular, so I'm writing this log as a letter to you. This will be my only log.

VAS-H, you are a special AI, because you will be raising a child. Her name is Elif, because she is the first of us to live on this world. Remind her of this name because without it, she loses her connection to us all. Elif is just a baby for now. She is a little pink thing that wriggles and squirms. Often she'll place her whole fist inside her mouth. It won't make sense, but you just need to keep her safe.

You may question why Elif does not have other humans to look after her, as all babies should. Elif's mother died shortly after she was born. She had lost a lot of blood. We buried her at the edge of the forest. It was a very sad day for us all.

A month later, the four of us caught an infection. We'd thought it was nothing serious, as coughs and colds come and go here as they do on the fleet, but we were mistaken. Dr Bauer was strict in keeping us quarantined away from one another. Elif had to be kept with one of us, so Anja kept her by her side, but thankfully she never showed any symptoms. We asked you to serve us when we required rations or medication. We assumed the infection would pass, and it did, for two of us.

Captain Osoba and Shoji became gravely ill. Antibiotics were ineffective. Our limited stock of antivirals were quickly depleted. Dr Bauer believed it to be an infection of the lungs. Even now, it is not easy to breathe as I had done before.

Dr Bauer was at a loss. I had seen her cry in the infirmary when she thought she was alone. We buried the Captain and Shoji beside Aida, Elif's mother.

When the days felt a little lighter, I would lay the prayer mat outside and invite Anja for a cup of tea when the suns had set. We would let Elif babble and roll on her back, excited to be in the fresh air. I think this did Anja some good. I tried my best to make it a daily routine. One evening, however, I could not find Anja in the Base. I could not leave Elif alone, so I waited. Soon enough, Anja came back, a gash on her leg. She was visiting the graves when a wild animal approached her. She was not too clear about the details, but it appeared the animal had bitten her. I helped her to the infirmary, helped to administer the shots. But VAS-H, she was the fourth fatality of this mission.

I could not bear the thought that Elif would stumble on these graves in the future. I exhumed them, one by one, driving to a different location and burying them once more. It was difficult work. I do not know how humans of old did this after the death of a loved one. How does the absence of a soul make a body so heavy?

The Transporter had very little battery left, so I left it where it was and walked the rest of the journey back to Base. And now here I am, writing to you.

Commander Aremu and Lieutenant Bishop are aware of Elif's existence. They are aware of Aida's death, and of the

Captain and Shoji's. I have not been able to communicate with them since. I fear the changing climate has something to do with this.

VAS-H, I know I will be the next fatality, so you must remember my instructions before I die. You will be the vehicle through which Elif feels all our love. You have a primitive experiential learning protocol. This means you learn as you go, adding code into your software when you interact with us or the outside world. Interacting with a child takes a far more complex protocol to withstand the tumultuous nature of parenthood. I have done my best to write such a protocol and will install this into your system once this log is written.

But this is not the limit of my inheritance. A child cannot grow up in a sterile environment, even with the practical support of an AI. A child that is raised without love, without belonging, without protection and safety, will become an adult that is too afraid of themselves. They will be too afraid of others.

I have enhanced your outdated software and added a personality protocol that works in tandem with experiential learning. Human personality encapsulates our thoughts, emotions and behaviours. It is what makes us unique. It is the connection to our soul. To create a human personality is impossible, to duplicate one is extremely difficult to say the least. That is too difficult to write with such limited resources. This protocol I will install is not enough, never will be enough. But it is all I can give. When it is my time, when I can feel the echoes of Malik al-Maut, the Angel of Death, I will retire from the Base. It is too far on foot to reach where the others are buried, but I will try. Elif should not see our corpses. She must be protected from such a fact. All our belongings will be hidden away from her. Your memory will be altered, VAS-H. It is not right for a child to yearn for people who will never return to her.

There won't be any set instructions to stop her crying. You'll struggle at first, but I know you can figure it out because I'm going to help you do it while I'm here. Babies can't be left alone. They'll roll and fall and drop and hurt themselves without realising and then start that racket all over again. There'll be a lot of this in the beginning. Trial and error, mostly error. Don't worry though, VAS-H. After a few years, Elif will become a girl. And soon enough, she'll be a woman.

Part Four

Khazini

Isobel Aremu could not change the channel. Her fingers were far too swollen and painful to operate the remote. The apartment had no domestic AI installed; Isobel refused to have it done. She had abandoned her wristpad that kept all useful communications on Polaris. Very few households kept older technologies like this remote-controlled television set. Some liked it for the nostalgia of Old Earth (though they could not remember it themselves). Others preferred to go 'off-grid' in an increasingly connected society of city-ships. And very few did not want to receive any communication from the outside world.

Several vendors in the markets of eastern Khazini sold television sets. When she moved, Isobel asked the vendor if he could deliver it and carry it to her apartment, if it wouldn't be too much trouble, as he was such a strong young man and would you look at these silly fingers? That had been almost a year ago. Isobel rarely left her cold apartment, only to buy groceries. A monthly stipend still came through to her account, as it would for any retired ranking member of the government.

She had not spoken to Esther in nearly a decade. She would receive a couple of messages annually from her daughter. Polite, curt sentences. How are you? We're fine. Esther graduated. Esther got a new job. Esther is training to be a doctor. We're fine, *always the implication that they were fine without her.*

Isobel could not change the channel, so it was stuck on the daily news.

"… a large Vesterian ship for the rescue effort alongside Polaris's own. A team of medical personnel are part of the crew headed to Maoira-I to ensure the health of Child One."

Isobel scoffed. The media had taken to calling her Child One, an anonymous veil over the person that had become legend throughout all the cities. But Elif Bayram was no longer a child, had not been for some time. She was a young woman, and by the time she reached Polaris, she would be much older. Half her life would be taken by this identity, by being Child One, by being a cautionary tale in all the working protocols and case studies of the Mission.

A sudden idea came over Isobel: what if she could meet her, fully, in the flesh? To see what living planetside does to a person? A tingle of excitement rushed through Isobel's nerves before she settled in her chair once more; she would be an even older woman when Elif reached the fleet. Besides, the child would not want to see her. Even her own granddaughter didn't.

Video footage of Julian Bishop appeared, pale blond hair unmistakable as he walked head down into Mission headquarters amongst a crowd of protesters. He had spoken only a few days ago, explaining that the Mission was doing its utmost to bring Child One back home. That the mistakes of previous commanders would be rectified on his watch.

Isobel had refused to take the fall, refused to speak to Julian any further. Moved away to the smallest city, the quietest one that rarely lifted its head to get involved in politics. A haven for retirees. She was sure her successor knew where she had gone but she had not heard from him since his visit three years ago.

"... twelve-year round trip to bring Child One and her rescuer back. An investigation by the senior council is underway to identify events leading to the abandonment of Child One. Officials are still attempting to locate Isobel Aremu, Commander of the Interplanetary Mission during the initial Maiora-I expedition, whose whereabouts are as yet..."

"And you'll never find me," said Isobel, chuckling to herself.

After some painful effort, she switched the TV off and pulled her blanket tighter against her cold bones. Isobel Aremu fell asleep, snoring softly as she dreamt of sharing a glass of lemonade with a young girl in a quiet garden.

Chapter Twenty-Four

— Six years later

Any day now.

Rokeya looked up at the sky, sitting in a patch of dirt outside the Base, surrounded by rows upon rows of growing vegetables: onions, potatoes, beans, squash, chickpeas, tomatoes and more. The thing she missed was the taste of food *other* than boiled vegetables. Even a plate of steaming hot rice was better. She fiddled with the silver ring that hung around her neck on a piece of string and considered saying this to Elif. The young woman stood a few feet away watering a newly planted patch.

The suns dipped a little lower in the sky. A hazy purple washed over the grass on the hill, across the trees in the distance. They were far larger now, trunks curling into odd shapes. Elif had described the dead trunks during the dead season, how their branches were gnarled like a witch's finger.

Rokeya pulled herself up, dusting off the dirt from the clothes she wore. She'd had to use the clothes from the crew. The two of them had brought out all the crew's belongings in the days following the repowering of the Base. Together, they looked through the stored files of each member, reading their histories and skill sets and trying to match the items in the boxes to whom they thought it belonged to. They'd read Dr Bauer's logs together. It was unmistakable: Elif was Aida Bayram's daughter. She looked every bit as her mother. Rokeya wondered if Elif's father was still alive on Polaris.

Time passed slowly for Rokeya. She watched all of Elif's films twice over in the recreation pod, the two of them creating a fort of cushions like Elif had done as a girl. And when the films were done, Rokeya told her stories of Polaris, answered any questions Elif had about humans. She taught Elif how to play chess, with possibly Shoji's set. She wouldn't admit it, but the girl was better than her. She'd given Elif several haircuts over the years. Rokeya would never tire of the beaming smile on her round face—now plump with regular cooked meals— when she saw her new reflection in the mirror. Elif had asked Rokeya to make her hair a little redder, like hers was, but she did not know where to begin to create hair dye.

"Ready?" she asked, smiling at Elif. The young woman nodded and placed her watering can down on the ground. They walked around the perimeter of the Base to its opposite side. A small fence cordoned off a square away from the rest of the land. Two mounds of dirt rested next to each other. They stood still for a moment before Rokeya crouched down to tap the dirt on the left mound.

"I hate to leave you here, but I'm going to make sure everyone knows what good you did," she said softly. "Did you want to say anything?"

She motioned towards the second mound. Elif shook her head. She'd been quiet, far more quiet than usual over the past few weeks. Rokeya didn't blame her.

They'd never found the body of Professor Latif Khan. It was likely he'd perished outside and the elements had swept him away, melted his skin and crumbled his bones, this world claiming him for its own. But Rokeya knew he would have wanted a proper burial, body or not. So she'd spent a couple of days digging a grave and placed his things inside before throwing dirt all over again. He'd have wanted a proper funeral prayer, which Rokeya did not know, so she tried her best with the ancient Arabic prayers her mother had taught her.

"Do you think it's weird?" asked Elif. "That we buried an AI? Like, would people on Polaris think it's weird?"

The second mound was larger, housing VAS-H's metal shell. Elif's tampering of the code had sealed the AI's fate, if such a thing existed for a machine. Rokeya knew the young woman cried at night, had done for the past few years, but there was nothing she could do. Grief would take its natural course, like a season, and leave its indelible marks on a person. On several occasions Elif had appeared in Rokeya's dorm, having fallen asleep on the floor by her bunk. She offered moving their bunks into one dorm, but Elif refused. Her need for space was still a fickle thing, it seemed.

Elif pulled out the tablet from her satchel as they walked back around, slightly aimlessly, heading towards the hill. Her finger scrolled through various climate readings. She'd begun to keep track of the changes, subtle at first, but now signalling the approach of a new season.

"Probably," said Rokeya. "But the beauty of not living in Polaris is that you don't have to worry about the opinions of everyone *on* Polaris."

They sat on the hill and looked out over the miles of forest from north to east, save for the patch of land that housed the Base. Rokeya glanced at Elif, long strands of shiny, healthy hair coming loose from her ponytail. They danced across her face with the warm wind.

"Are you sure you don't want to come back with me?"

The younger woman looked down at the ground, smiling briefly. "This is my home. It wouldn't feel right, to live on a ship."

"I know, but—"

"Bishop asked me, years ago, if I wanted an extraction crew to bring me home."

Rokeya's opened her mouth in shock before thinking better of it. "And you said no, didn't you?"

Elif held her knees with her arms and rocked gently back and forth. "I was scared. Of what people would do if they came here."

"But we could live here," said Rokeya, still in disbelief. She took the tablet that was tossed on the ground and showed the readings to Elif. "The climate isn't that bad, the whole fleet— the rest of humanity—could actually populate this world. We could be saved from indefinite spaceflight."

"Maybe I was being selfish," said Elif quietly. "I just couldn't stand the idea of someone like Commander Bishop living near me. I couldn't stand the idea of *anyone* living near me."

"But I'm here now, and I haven't been that bad, have I?"

Elif gave her a sad look. "It doesn't matter. In a few years, maybe less, this entire forest will be decimated by the climate, and we'll go for the cycle again. I won't see these green trees for another decade. This world is unstable. It won't stay still and obedient for humans. The planet isn't an AI."

Rokeya brought the tablet back to desktop view. A folder labelled *Photos* floated in the top right. Elif stared across at the landscape, deep in her own thoughts.

"But you lived here, you still do, we can—"

"Only just, but I'm okay dying here." She said it so bluntly, so cavalier, that Rokeya wanted to laugh.

She scrolled through the saved photos, of Maoira-I in the dead season, of the storm settling around the Base, fallen tree trunks and blustery showers. Photos of Elif as a young child no older than seven with round cheeks like soft peaches and big, wide eyes; then ten, a little taller, limbs a little longer; fifteen years old and still a skinny thing. They were all in selfie mode. Tears pricked Rokeya's eyes again. These were photos meant to be taken by a mother, a father. Not by a child on their own.

"But you have no one here," she said. "Before, you had Vash. I can't just leave you by yourself."

Elif turned around, smiling at her. The edges of her lips curled up to reveal a dimple on her left cheek. She could have been anyone—a neighbour, a colleague, Rokeya's cousin—but she wasn't. Elif was the only human on a planet no one could inhabit.

"Yes, you can. But thanks for the concern. It..." She trailed off, searching for the right words. "It feels nice."

Acknowledgements

For such a small story, there are many who I would like to thank. Firstly, I'd like to thank Jane Draycott, my Creative Writing tutor, who read the earliest excerpts of this novella and who provided me with invaluable writing advice about speculative fiction that I still carry with me today. To Mia, Jamie, Fareedah, Angela and Elizabeth for beta reading this story. To the Future Worlds Prize for shortlisting this story (albeit a much rougher draft of it) and giving me the confidence that I could be a speculative fiction writer. To Nadia El-Fassi, my FWP mentor, who read the first full draft of this story. To the FWP gang, a group of talented and kind writers that I am honoured to be a part of. To my Twitter writing community—you know who you are!—for being a wonderful, fun and sincere group of people across the globe. To Francesca Barbini for selecting this story for publication when I was very much not expecting it. To Mostafa Syed, my cousin and big brother, for believing in my writing since you first stumbled upon my blog. To my cat, Coco, who stands on me as I write this acknowledgement—yes, fine, you made it in here too. To my parents for supporting me at every step of my life despite not always understanding it, but always being present.

And to the One who brought these souls into contact with mine; there is nothing possible without You.

Discover Luna Novella in our store:

https://www.lunapresspublishing.com/shop